William Forsell Kirby

Ed-Dimiryaht

An Oriental Romance and Other Poems

William Forsell Kirby

Ed-Dimiryaht
An Oriental Romance and Other Poems

ISBN/EAN: 9783337049744

Printed in Europe, USA, Canada, Australia, Japan

Cover: Foto ©Andreas Hilbeck / pixelio.de

More available books at **www.hansebooks.com**

PREFACE.

It is so long since an Oriental poem of any pretensions, (not a translation) has been published, that it is impossible to say if such a work is likely to be popular or otherwise; but no one will deny that the mythology of the whole East, especially of India, Persia, and Arabia, presents a vast mine of almost untouched poetic wealth.

Lane's system of writing Oriental names is employed throughout, excepting only accents, which would be inadmissible in a work of this nature. I have, however, though somewhat inaccurately, substituted for the accented "a", "o", and "s", "ah", "oh", and "ss", except in a few cases in which it seemed to be unnecessary. Words not occurring in Lane's works, are also written as closely as possible according to his system. In the Notes, all the names are written without accents; and as they are spelt by the authors from whose writings they are taken. Some will perhaps blame me for not adopting a more familiar method of spelling than Lane's; but in default of a standard uniform system, I preferred to use one which is at least sanctioned by high authority. I have avoided the use of such terms as "Genii" and "Fairies", to obviate the confusion of ideas always caused by transferring the names of the spirits of one mythology to those of another.

The legendary portion of the poem (books 3 and 4) might have been enlarged to any extent; and while in some cases (b. 3, c. 2, aud b. 4. c. 1, for example), the original story has been little deviated from, in other cases, the legends have been embellished, and, at the same time, abridged, as is the case with b. 3, c. 8.

It is very difficult always to avoid imitating a previous author; or sometimes even to be certain whether imitation exists in two parallel passages, or not. Where I have suspected that any existed, I have either carefully expunged the passage, or referred to the apparent original in a note. Nevertheless, extracts from poems are frequently quoted rather as illustrations than as acknowledgments. Whether I can fairly be accused of plagiarism when every line where I suspected I might be influenced by another author has been acknowledged, I do not know; but occasional imitation within certain limits is sanctioned by the highest authorities; and several of the most eminent poets have been the greatest imitators.

Although the imagery of the poem is Eastern, the prevailing tone is probably Western. The notes are purposely as short as possible, being only intended to explain the text, without encumbering it. The needless multiplication of references is also avoided. I have not thought it necessary to append more than an occasional brief introductory Note to the shorter Poems.

"Alcyone," the second longest poem in the volume, was originally commenced at the suggestion of a scientific friend, but I found myself quite unable to carry out his idea on the gigantic scale first contemplated. The astronomical theories and speculations there referred to, are employed as part of the machinery, without any intention to imply their exact scientific accuracy.

Two of the shorter poems at the end of the volume, "Thalassa", and "The Poet", have already appeared in the "Social Science Review" for 1865.

I have not published these poems hastily, as they have all undergone careful revision; and, in particular, "Ed-Dimiryaht" represents much of the labour of some years. No one can object to his work being freely criticised; and fairness in all that an author is justified in demanding of his critics.

W. F. Kirby.

CONTENTS.

~~~~~~

ED-DIMIRYAHT.

BOOK THE FIRST.

THE KINGDOM OF JINNEESTAHN.

ARGUMENT.

I. The Seventh Earth. Iblees and his followers. His Defiance. His troops build him a palace. Descent of his family. They swear allegiance to him. Ed-Dimiryaht and Marjahneh refuse. Marjahneh imprisoned. Escape of Ed-Dimiryaht. Iblees sends his sons to summon a general assembly of the Kings of the Jinn. Zelemboor commissioned to pursue Ed-Dimiryaht.

II. Ed-Dimiryaht ascends to Heaven. Appearance of Azraeel. Their flight to the Throne of God. Repulse of Zelemboor. The Archangels. God sends Ed-Dimiryaht to the Seventh Earth with the Sword of Azraeel.

III. Speeches of Iblees and Ed-Dimiryaht. The kings form two parties. Iblees attachs Ed-Dimiryaht, but only loses the arms of Jarjarees. Marjahneh and Dahsim. Repulse of Iblees and his army. Ed-Dimiryaht escapes to the earth with his followers.

IV.   Mount Kahf. Ed Dimiryaht founds the Kingdom of Jinneestahn. Marjahneh becomes his wife. Azraeel reclaims his sword.
Its hidden properties. The glories of Jinneestahn. The vain attempts
of Iblees to invade the country.

CANTO I

THE DESIGNS OF IBLEES.

WHERE, son of Jarjarees, [1] is now thy home?
How canst thou dwell in either Earth or Heaven
Beneath the curse of God? Material force
Is needed not to drive thee to an earth [2]
The lowest of the Seven, where God decrees   5
Thou shalt await thy doom till time is o'er.
The light of Heaven, or e'en the light of Earth,
Thy proud, ungrateful spirit cannot bear,
But needs a world of everlasting gloom,
Whose dreary horrors may benumb despair.   10
Ungrateful wretch to wreak thy wrath on men, [3]
Since God a portion af His boundless love
Lavished on them! Supposest thou that God
Loved thee the less because he made a race
Superior, yet inferior to thy own!   15
     For countless ages lay the Seventh Earth,
A cheerless desert racked by fearful storms.
Barren alike was hill and plain and sea,
For never shines a ray af heavenly light,
On worlds that lie beneath the highest earth.   20
The light may touch, but may not chase their gloom:
An awful twilight can but half reveal

The horrors of those worlds. The Seventh Earth,
All desolation in itself combines,
For neither beast nor herb nor tree can bear   25
The deadly gas that issues from its soil.
Angels and Jinn⁴ have ever shunned a world
So desolate! A fearful mystery
Has hung around it long, for angels ask,
"Why should so desolate a region be?"   30
    At length a troop of angels and of Jinn
Approach the fearful spot, and cleave and hew
The mountains' rugged sides, and with the rocks
Rear a stupendous hall; but o'er the hall,
A cloud of gloom no splendour might dispel,   35
(If splendour on the palace e'er might rest,)
Is brooding, and a sad and evil look
Hangs o'er the palace. There they reared a throne
For him who led them here to share his woe,
And seats that suited well the council-hall,   40
Composed of rocks from out the mountains hewn.
    Behold their Leader where he stands apart
While they complete the work, a mass of rock
Grasped in his hand with such convulsive force,
As furious thoughts come surging through his brain, 45
That e'en the rock is crushed. He heeds it not,
But recklessly he hurls around the flames ⁵
That well proclaim him of the race of Jinn,
Heedless of all things save the unwonted cares,
And the presumptuous thoughts that rage within,   50
And goad him on to evil, while they brand
The scars of pride and cruelty and wrath
Deep in his brow; and these the Zakkoom ⁶ juice
Alone shall cleanse away. At length he spoke,

Crushing the stone to powder in his hand,   55
And gazing upward with a hideous scowl.
  ' Tyrant, the sons of Flame stoop not to Earth!
If, Allah, thou wouldst once again receive
El Hahrith into favour, did he kneel
To Adam, he would spurn indignantly   60
The tempting offer! Hast thou made a race
Superior to the Jinn? Behold, they fell
Before the first temptation! Are not these
Above the angels, and above the Jinn?
El Hahrith has o'ercome thee! Vainly curse   65
Thy conquering slave who now defies thy power!
El Hahrith shall destroy the puny race
Thou dotest thus upon; nor stops he here,
For all the Jinn and all the angels too
Shall join his host of heroes, and at length   70
Shall teach thee that El Habrith ne'er forgives
A conquered enemy!"
               The Jinnee ceased
His impious speech, and quenching first his flames,
Approached the palace with unsteady steps,
While plain appeared the tumult in his soul,   75
Convulsing all his frame with bootless rage.
Too proud was Iblees to perceive his state,
But in his heart he felt all peace was gone.
How dread soever outward pains may be,
Jahennem's flames and Zakkoom burn within,   80
And not without, a sinner. Iblees felt
How true was this, but stifled the despair
That well might warrant now his altered name,
And when he reached the hall his troops had built,
Mounted the throne, and gazed upon the Jinn.   85

The sons of Iblees [7] when their father fell,
Among themselves debated were it best
To stay in heaven, or call their children round
And seek to learn his fate? The latter course
So forcibly was urged by Teer, that all   90
Bowed to his judgement, sending through the heavens,
Their messengers to call the favoured Jinn
Who dwelt among the angels. Some there were,
Who ventured to upraise a warning voice,
But these were overruled, and all agreed   95
To follow Iblees to the Seventh Earth,
And learn the upshot of his fatal sin.
When Iblees saw his sons, a look of joy
And evil triumph flashed across his face,
And speaking not, he bade the guards by sign   100
To part their ranks, dividing right and left,
Until his sons should stand before his throne,
And close behind them. Iblees rose and stood,
Prepared to force his sons to share his doom,
Still on his face the look of fiendish joy,   105
When from his brow the withered lote-tree wreath [8]
Fell to the ground, the fadeless leaves of heaven
Blackened and blasted by the rebel's sin!
He saw the portent: swift he turned away
To hide his face from all who near him stood.   110
Dismayed and deadly sick at heart he felt,
For well he understood the awful sign,
And knew that God had left him to himself.
But quickly Iblees turned and faced his troops,
And seizing franticly the withered leaves,   115
He cast them in the air, and cried aloud,
"Behold me cast away the leaves of Heaven!

So cast I Allah from me, he whose power
Depends on me. I now withdraw my aid,
And fall he must. He thinks himself a king.   120
A king indeed! He cares so much for ease,
That evermore he sits upon his throne,
To view the shining worlds that lie beneath!
To slaves who toil for him, he trusts his worlds,
(And chiefly to myself in former years)   125
And now I serve him not, his worlds must sink
In darkness. I will hurl him off the throne,
Whereon myself I placed him. He shall know
El Hahrith is his enemy, for ne'er
To him I'll kneel again. The human race,   130
Which Allah calls superior to ourselves,
Will we destroy. My sons, I call on you
To aid me in my righteous enterprise,
But if you will not greet me as your king,
My troops shall slay you. In my hand you are,   135
And I must weaken and destroy the force
Of Allah at whatever points I can,
Though I may seem to act against myself."
    They looked around them when they heard his words,
But could not now escape; and one by one   140
The sons of Iblees knelt before his throne,
And 'mid the army's acclamations, swore
Eternal enmity to God and man.
    Then Iblees spoke again, "Before my throne,
Let my descendants kneel and own my power,   145
And let them take the oath of emnity
To God and all his creatures. I am king!
Yes; Allah would have slain me if he could,
But he perceived that 'twas beyond his power,

So when to Adam I refused to kneel,　　　　150
He granted me a respite to repent!
How I despise his folly! He has lost
His chance of ever crushing me.　Ye know
My father Jarjarees opposed his might,
And 'twas the fault of treason if he failed　　155
To slay the tyrant.　When my father fell,
The angels made me prisoner.　I have served
The conqueror till he thought to make me kneel
Before a thing of earth.　An army flocked
Around my standard, and I led them here,　　160
And they shall tear the tyrant from his throne,
And drag him to my feet, when I'll inflict
On him the tortures he reserves for me!"
　　And were there none who dared to face the Chief?
Did all his weak descendants bow the knee　　165
Before the rebel Iblees? Many knelt,
And took the fearful oath; but two there were
Who stood alone amid the abject crowd.
One was an Efreet who had long been known
To be the most unwearied of his race,　　170
In every task assigned him when in Heaven.
Though Ed-Dimiryaht⁹ was Zelemboor's son,
And though Zelemboor first of all had knelt
Before his father Iblees, he would stoop
To none but Allah.　Ed-Dimiryaht came,　　175
In hope that he might lead to God again
The rebel army.　In succeeding years,
Was Dahsim known as fiercest of the sons
Of Iblees, yet his youngest daughter stood
By Ed-Dimiryaht only.　Iblees spoke,　　180
But scarcely could repress the rage he felt,

Sufficiently to vent his wrath in words.
"Have all your kindred knelt before my throne,
And yet you think I'll brook a sight like this?
Your fathers have acknowledged me as king,   185
And ye, shall ye oppose your rightful Lord?
Slaves, would you serve a tyrant who commands
The sons of fire to stoop to things of earth?
'Tis water, 'tis not flame that fills your veins!
Must I enforce submission by my troops,   190
Or will you yield to me? You did not hear
My proclamation rightly, or supposed
That I addressed my army? Yield to me,
And I will honour you above the rest,
But if you will not hear me, you shall die."   195
    Zelemboor rose. "Permit me, King, to speak. —
You cannot stand against El Hahrith's might,
And, Ed-Dimiryaht, I myself have bowed
To his decrees. His wrath is swift and sure.
Appease it while you may. The Seventh Earth   200
Is dark and far from Heaven, and Allah's eyes
Can never pierce its darkness. You may thus
Remain in Heaven, and work my father's will,
While Allah thinks you serve him. Thus may you
Obtain rewards from both the rival Kings."   205
    "And thus by serving neither, both deceive!"
Said Ed-Dimiryaht gently, though his face
Was sad and steadfast in its firm resolve.
He mourned for those who bowed to Iblees down,
But every moment bolder he became,   210
And firmer to resist El Hahrith's wrath,
And those deceitful words Zelemboor spoke.
"Yes, Allah can preserve us from your might!

El Hahrith, two acknowledge not your power,
And though we stand alone, the might of God   215
Surrounds us here, invisible to all.
His eye can penetrate the darkest night,
And do not think that he beholds us not,
And do not hope to 'scape his awful might.
Alas, O friends, will none among you all   220
Submit to Allah?"
                              More he wished to say,
But Dahsim to Marjahneh's [10] side had sprung,
And loud his voice resounded through the hall.
"Marjahneh, traitress, wherefore still resolve
To serve a king like Allah? Well were it   225
To kneel before El Hahrith, and beseech
His pardon for your fault, or you shall feel
The greatest punishment within his power,
Although you are my daughter, do not think
That I shall intercede for you with him.   230
Zelemboor has explained how you may best
Escape the anger of the rival kings.
'Tis best to yield and bow before my sire,
And then return to Heaven, and there pretend
You now opposed him. Then you oft may thwart   235
The plans of Allah, fearing not that he
Your treachery will perceive. I give you now
My counsel, O Marjahneh, and command
That you obey me!"
                              Then Marjahneh shrank
Back from her father, yet she would not stoop   240
To Iblees, who was writhing on his throne
In speechless rage and fury, while the troops
Looked with respectful silence on the scene.

At leugth Marjahneh thus to Dahsim spoke,
A calm determination in her face,   245
Resolved to oppose El Hahrith and his friends.
"Alas, my father, wherefore must I bow
Before El Hahrith? Dare you call him God?
He did not make me what I am. I yield
To none but Allah, and hypocrisy,   250
If any dared to act that shameful part,
He must at once perceive. His arm shall save
Both Ed-Dimiryaht and myself from those
Who cringe before a rebel."
                              Once again
Spoke Ed-Dimiryaht, but he now addressed   255
The rebel army. "Hear me, I demand!
Do you not feel that innocence is gone,
And happiness is fled for evermore?
If you return to Allah, hope remains,
But should you aid El Hahrith's ill designs,   260
The punishments that Allah's mercy grants
To lead you to himself, I dare not say.
They will not be severer than your sins
Have earned; but pray for pardon from your King,
Nor longer dare offend him. O return   265
To virtue and to God, while time remains!"
    But Iblees now could speak, and up he sprang, .
And dashed his iron sceptre to the ground,
And shivered it to pieces in his rage,
So that the splinters flew to evrey wall.   270
"What, yield to Allah! Never, though I lay
Beneath the Sword of Azraeel! 11 Ne'er again ·
Will I submit to be his slave, and toil
To please a tyrant! Ye who hear my words,

Remove the traitors from before my sight,   275
Lay them in chains and guard them. They shall feel
My wrath amid the whole assembled race
Of Jinn. I loathe the sight of those who seek
To please a tyrant, a destested wretch,
Whom I abhor and utterly renounce,   280
And whom I now abandon evermore!"
    The guards closed round their victims, dragged them
                                                    forth,
And 'mid the mountains led them. First they seized
Marjahneh, who resisted not her foes,
But closed her eyes, and clasped her hands and prayed 285
They cast Marjahneh down, and o'er her piled
A mighty heap of rocks. The guards stepped back,
And seized an Ed-Dimiryaht, but he cried,
"Marjahneh, fear not. I will fly to Heaven,
And tear you from El Hahrith's wrath unscathed." 290
    He spoke, and as he spoke, a sheet of flame
That lighted all the gloomy hills around,
Descended on his fadeless wreath of lote.
The guards sprang back confounded, while he rose
Above them, veiled in light they could not bear,   295
Nor had the band the courage to pursue,
Till he was far away, and soon he reached
The earth above, and this he cleft in twain,
And vanished from his base pursuers' sight.
The baffled guards beheld with shame and rage,   300
And thus their leader spoke: "We will not quit
The Seventh Earth, for sure our foe has fled
Back to the Heaven that he has never lost.
We cannot overtake him, we are armed,
And he has nought that might impede his flight,   305

And if we overtook him, who would face
A Jinnee, whom the King we dare not name,
So openly protects? I will not risk
A further conflict with him. We must go,
And must acquaint El Hahrith with his flight."   310
Slowly they turned their flight to earth again,
Each blaming all the others, downcast, sad,
And dreading most of all to face their King.
     Meantime El Harith thus addressed his slaves.
"I wish to call the mighty Kings who rule   315
The race of Jinn who dwell beneath the heavens.
They surely cannot now refuse to grant
The universal empire of the race,
To me, the son of Jarjarces, the last,
And greatest of the Kings to whom they bowed,   320
Ere Allah in his folly made mankind.
Dahsim, Zelemboor, Soht, El Aawar, Teer,
My faithful sons, command the Jinnee Kings
To meet the son af Jarjarees, and crown
Successor to him, one whom they shall deem   325
Most worthy of the honour. I have here
His crown, his arms, his treasures. In my hall,
When every monarch of the Jinn attends,
Shall Ed-Dimiryaht and Marjahneh feel
My utmost wrath."   330
              As Iblees spoke, the guards,
Rushed in confusion to his throne, and cried,
"El Hahrith, Ed-Dimiryaht has escaped!"
But he continued, "Seek the traitor out,
Zelemboor, till you find him, yet beware.
Above the Seventh Heaven you may not soar, [12]   335
For only Allah's faithful ones have power

To reach his Throne, o'erarching all the Heavens."
"I hear and I obey!" Zelemboor cried,
"And I will bring my son to suffer all
That you can heap on his devoted head.   340
I marvel much that he should meanly fear
The wrath of Allah, which you well may know
Expends itself in empty threats alone.
Did Adam die, or Eve, upon the day
When first they tasted the forbidden vine? [13]   345
Nay, and Jahennem is an idle tale,
And we shall never suffer punishment
For what it pleases God to term our sins!"
      Swift to the earth, the highest of the seven,
The sons of Iblees rose. They bade the Kings   350
Attend the summons of the son of him
Who ruled them last, to choose another Chief;
And all the Kings obeyed.
                              Zelemboor searched
The Seven Earths in vain to find his son;
Then bade his brothren to their father's realms   355
Descend with all the Kings, while he should search
The Seven Heavens. He thought within himself,
"El Hahrith has forwarned me that the wings
Of those who dare 'gainst Allah to rebel,
May ne'er approach his Throne; but nought I care 360
For this; and if I find not else my son,
I'll drag him from before the Throne itself,
And all the angels may in vain oppose."
      Zelemboor, knowest thou not that thou art weak,
As wickedness must ever find itself?   365
Aye, thou mayest seek thy son, but thou shalt learn
No evil power shall ever crush him down! [11]

CANTO II.

ED-DIMIRVAHT IN HEAVEN.

WHEN Ed-Dimiryaht left his foes afar,
And reached the boundaries of the Seventh Earth,
He checked his speed and feared pursuit no more   370
But did not cease his upward flight for that,
Until he hovered o'er the highest Earth,
Which shone with life and beauty, for the clouds
Enhanced the radiance of the summer sun,
And rarely veiled it with their fleecy folds.   375
As yet the foot of man had scarcely touched
The virgin sod. It seemed as God himself,
Had planted o'er the earth a garden fair,
Where no decay could injure or destroy.
Well might the Jinnee as he gazed exclaim: 380
"How beautiful this earth which lies below!
O surely God is merciful to grant
So bright a home to Adam and to Eve, [15]
Although they disobeyd his high commands,
And lost the Heaven in which he placed them first! 385
Here will I dwell, — my race is made for Earth:
They cannot yet endure the bliss of Heaven,
And like mankind they also yield to sin.
But here on earth may Allah's work be done,
And Heaven be won by waiting. Would to God,   390
I might induce El Hahrith here to dwell,
And bow before his rightful Lord again!
I must confront El Hahrith in his pride,
And wrest Marjahneh from the Evil Jinn.
Against the Jinn the Heavens are never closed,   395

And I have never sinned against my God,
And He who saved me once will aid me now."
  He turned and left the earth and soaring up,
He reached the portals of the lowest Heaven,
And unopposed he passed the open gate.   400
The angels who beheld him thronged around :
"A messenger from lower worlds has come,
Not one of us, but sprung from smokeless fire.
Say on what mission sent you sought the earth,
And what success was your's?"
                   But one who knew   405
The Jinnee, thus addressed him: "Come you not,
Son of Zelemboor, from the Seventh Earth ?
Unwithered still is your celestial wreath;
By that we know you have not joined the Fiend.
Were you the only faithful one who dared   410
Against El Hahrith's counsels raise his voice?
If others spoke against him, it is strange
That you alone have sought your ancient home."
  Then Ed-Dimiryaht mournfully replied,
"Marjahneh only dared with me oppose   415
El Hahrith. She is laid in chains; and here
I come to seek assistance from your might."
  As with one voice the angels all exclaimed,
"Should Allah not forbid it, every one
With you will seek the Seventh Earth, and face   420
The rebel host, nor dread El Hahrith's might;
Although there was a time when none would dare
To say a word against him. Great are those
Who fail not in temptation! They shall tread
The Bridge of Breadth[16] in safety! God be praised, 425
That all the race of Iblees is not lost!"

An angel, who had stood apart, and gazed
Far in the heavens, approached the throng, and stood,
His hand upraised, and pointing to the sky,
As he addressed his fellows : "See you not   430
In distant space, a beam of glorious light?
'Tis some Archangel sent from Allah's Throne
To Ed-Dimiryaht. — It is Azraeel's self,
The sternest, yet the mildest of our race,
Most pitiless and yet most merciful ;   435
'Tis he whose Sword shall dry· up every tear,
Right every wrong, and every holy joy
Restore. For no light purpose he descends
From where he sits before the Throne of God!
But swift he comes, and we shall shortly hear   440
The message which he brings us."
                                        Solemnly
They waited the Archangel. He was crowned
With lote-leaves like themselves, but mixed with these,
What are those tongues of lurid flame that glide
Amid his shining wreath? The Zakkoom leaves   445
Are twisted with the lote, the tree of Hell,
Thus mingling with the holiest tree of Heaven,
To crown the noblest form that ever yet
Had Ed-Dimiryaht seen. The angel's face
Was stern and calm; no passion could disturb   450
Its settled mournfulness, and yet his eyes
With holy joy were bright; and those who gazed
Might see all mysteries hidden in the depths
Of his dark eyes, so deep that none could read
Their meaning fully. They were as the sea,   455
Which far below that daring diver lay, [17]

Who plunged amid Charybdis' jaws of foam,
And who beheld the darkening gulf that slept
Unruffled by the breezes that above
Might play upon the happier, lighter waves: 460
Save where the mighty torrents rushed, unmoved
An awful gulf of inky purple hue.
The secrets dread concealed from human eye
That diver dared to pierce. Again he dived,
To win a peerless prize by braving Hell,   465
And he returned no more. As deep a gulf,
As fathomless as that the diver viewed,
Were Azraeel's wondrous eyes. O marvel not,
If he of all the angels never smiles!
Though his bright presence lightened Heaven around, 470
Yet his broad wings cast gloom where'er their shade
Fell on the ground. The angel swiftly flew
To those who still round Ed-Dimiryaht stood,
And presently alighting in the midst,
To Ed-Dimiryaht he addressed his words.   475
    "Son of Zelemboor, hast thou then alone
Resisted Iblees, and unharmed escaped
The dire contagion of thy evil house?
Have the celestial wreaths of all thy race
Faded, as that of Iblees? Were there none   480
To stand by thee? I scarcely can believe
That all the rest of Iblees' troops are lost:
But if there were among them those who feared
To pledge themselves the rebel's willing slaves,
Why sought they not with thee their ancient home?" 485
    Undazzled by the Archangel's glorious form,
Was Ed-Dimiryaht, as he made reply.
"Mightiest of angels, one beside me stood

Who would not stoop to Iblees. She awaits
The punishment his cruelty suggests,   490
In chains. O grant that even if too late
To warn El Hahrith to renounce his sins,
That I may seek again the Seventh Earth,
And wrest Marjahneh from the unpitying hosts!"
    He ceased, and Azraeel answered, "Do not hope 495
The power is thine to lead El Hahrith back!
Jahennem must receive the rebel Jinn,
Until their sins are wholly purged away. [18]
Thou yet art true, and though thou mayst approach
The Throne that arches o'er the Seventh Heaven,   500
Yet those who dare 'gainst Allah to rebel,
If they should strive to reach his awful Throne,
Would strike against a bar of adamant,
And chains would weigh them to the Seventh Earth.
But God himself shall teach thee how to act;   505
So seek with me his Throne."
                           He spoke, and sprang
Again into the air, but not alone,
For Ed-Dimiryaht followed, whilst the Heaven
Below them rushed away. It vanished soon,
And empty space above, below, around,   510
Spread far as eye could reach. Another Heaven
Above them arched, but Azraeel did not stay
Till in the Seventh Heaven he set his feet,
When he to Ed-Dimiryaht spoke again:
    "Above us yet the Throne of God is fixed,   515
More distant than the highest Heaven itself
Is from the lowest Earth. Around the Throne,
A blaze of light and glory infinite
Extends for ever. Thinkest thou thy wings

Can bear thee up before the Throne of God,   520
Or that thy eyes can bear the dazzling light?
If thou dost fear to seek the Throne thyself,
Await me here."
                    Again he sprang on high,
But Ed-Dimiryaht followed fearlessly.
Zelemboor vainly sought his son before   525
In lower Heavens, and closely now pursued
In fury, but he dashed with all his force
Against the barrier. He recoiled, amazed,
Yet, viewing no resistance, rushed again
To seize his son. Again he struck the bar,   530
And bands that none could break around him closed.
He tried to grasp the chains he could not see, —
They clung around till every limb was bound
And powerless. To the Seventh Earth he fell,
There all the chains were loosed, and he was left   535
Within the Hall of Iblees, whence he came,
A fitter place than Heaven or earth for him!
    "Behold my father!" Ed-Dimiryaht cried.
"I hoped that he at least in heart was true,
Yet has he fallen! The future's plain to thee: 540
Will he repent before the Trumpet sounds,
And will the bridge Siraht support his weight?"
    "Nay!" Azraeel answered, "surely in his heart,
Zelemboor has rebelled. The fearful bridge
Shall sink beneath the wicked. Thou shalt see   545
The troops of Iblees, when compelled to pass
The bridge, fall headlong in the gulf below.
But never shouldst thou yield unto despair!
Jahennem's flames are doomed to pass away.
This mayst thou know. Far, far above us still   550

Is placed the Throne of Allah: stay not here,
But follow where I lead."
                              The angel gazed
Amid the increasing light, and upward soared.
Sea after sea of light was left behind,
Till Azraeel rose amid ·the dazzling rays   555
That flash for ever round the Throne of God.
No longer Ed-Dimiryaht could endure
The glories round him: blinded by the light,
He faltered helpless 'mid the trackless sea,
And cried to Azraeel, "Save me or I fall!   560
The glories here are more than I can bear.
My eyes are closed with light, my wings are weak,
O save me, Azrael, or I helpless fall!"
     The angel Azraeel caught him as he fell,
And led him up before the Throne of God.   565
The Archangels sat upon their thrones in front,
And Azraeel took his seat, and in the midst
Set Ed-Dimiryaht, and addressed him thus:
"Jinnee, the eternal Throne at length is reached!
The glories which o'erwhelmed thee thou canst bear   570
Now that thou standest here. I wondered much
To see that thou couldst bear the light so long:
For e'en among the angels, few have faith
To face the splendour of the Throne of God.
But thou in thine integrity art strong,   575
And here thou standest. Raise thine eyes, and see
The sights that none save Iblees and thyself,
Of all thy race, though formed of smokeless flame,
Shall see till every prophecy's fulfilled!"
     He heard the words of Azraeel, and he fixed   580
His eyes upon the quenchless, dazzling light,

Which from the highest of created powers,
Conceals unheard-of wonders. But a sound
Came through the steady glory loud and clear,
A mighty throbbing. "Hearest thou", exclaimed   585
The angel Azraeel, "hearest thou the Heart
That sends the fluids which control the worlds,
Throughout the universe? Electric power,
And Odyle, most mysterious force of all,
By which the living and the dead converse,   590
And Light and Heat and many a force beside,
Are forms of that which lies behind them all,
And guides eternally the wheels of fate,
The subtle Fluid which controls the All,
And which thou well mayst hear the Heart of God   595
Propel throughout all Nature. — View the thrones
Where sit the Archangels."
                        Ed-Dimiryaht looked,
And saw where Azraeel sat. His throne was black,
A dull, dead blackness that reflected nought.
Above his head there hung the Sword of Death,   600
A Sword whose shining blade was quenchless flame,
Yet covered over with the drops of gall,
That give the sword its sharpness. Near it hung
The keys of every Heaven and every Hell.
    Awhile did Ed-Dimiryaht view his throne,   605
Then turned to that of Meekaeel. He beheld
A mighty angel on a blood-red throne.
The lofty sadness clouding Azraeel's brow;
Sat not on his. A proud and kingly air,
Denoting zeal and firmness, took its place.   610
His eyes were ever fixed upon the Throne,
As waiting some command. Above his head

The Jewish talismans were hung, the Rod
Of Moosa, [19] and Suleymahn's [20] mighty Seal.
    Milder than these sat Jebraeel on a throne   615
Whiter than snow. He held a pen of light,
And on the Table of Eternity [21]
He wrote the future history of the world.
Above his head the inspired books were hung
Which afterwards should be revealed to men.   620
The books of Moosa and Suleymahn's books,
And over all, the books which tell the life
Of Eesa. [22] But beside the o'ervalued books
Of Moosa and his followers, hung the Vedas,
And there the Zend-Avesta, the Kurahn,   5
The books which Homer, Milton, Shakspeare wrote,
And every other writing which has power
To lift the souls of men to things divine.
    Last of the four, but equal to the rest,
Israhfeel sat upon a glassy throne.   630
His restless eyes explored the brilliant light,
And ever sought to pierce its deepest depths.
Above his head the mighty Trumpet hung,
Which none but he shall sound. At length he felt
The light had reached his soul, and up he sprang, 635
And poured a flood of matchless melody,
Such as in Heaven he only has the power
To breathe, for of the angels only he
Has for his heartstrings a celestial lute. [23]

      "Away from all meaner splendours!   640
       Though bright are the worlds above,
     Far brighter the Throne before us,
       The Throne of Eternal Love.

I serve thee, O God, for ever,
  And thou unto me hast given   645
The trumpet whose thunder echoes
  To deepest of Hells from Heaven.

O, bright is the Throne of Glory
  Round which the Archangels kneel;
But what when the veil is lifted,   650
  And God shall Himself reveal?

The trumpet shall shake all regions,
  Jahennem itself shall fall:
When God has reclaimed the wicked,
  Then shall he be all in all!   655

The eyes of his faithfullest servants
  Can hardly endure the light
That circles the Throne for ever,
  To veil a more glorious sight.

O thou, who hast pierced the splendour   660
  That veileth His Throne adored!
Approach to the light unfearing,
  And call on thy chosen Lord!

O thou of the race of Iblees,
  Whose faith is as great as ours!   665
So great be thy faith for ever, —
  The wonder of all good powers!

Come forward, O Ed-Dimiryaht,
  Where few but thyself dare stand,
And call on the God of Nature,   670
  And trust in his mighty hand!"

He ceased, and Ed-Dimiryaht forward came,
And spoke: "Eternal Lord of Heaven and Earth,
Grant me to lead my grandsire back to thee,
Or if this may not be, at least I ask   675
For power to snatch the faithful from the hands
Of those who have rebelled, and thee blasphemed!"

The Jinnee bent his head before the Throne,
And lo, in answer came a solemn Voice
That thrilled through all his frame; and on their knees 680
The Archangels fell in reverence: "True to God
Thou art, and ever shalt be. Not for thee,
Is it to call El Hahrith from his sins:
But thou mayst warn his followers. While I speak,
The rebel calls the Kings of all the Jinn,   685
To choose a ruler. Some will side with him,
But whomsoe'er 'tis granted thee to save,
At once shall greet thee King. To Heaven itself,
Thou mayst not lead thy followers, till the time
When the Third Trumpet sounds, though thou thyself 690
Mayst freely enter here. Thy kingdom found
Where mighty Kahf [24] encircles all the sea
Which flows around the highest of the earths.
Approach no more the accursed Seventh Earth,
When once thy faithful bands have left its bounds, 695
Except when I command thee. Take the Sword
Of Azraeel. Draw the sword and wave it round,
And all thy foes shall fall before its flash,
Dazzled and senseless."
                            Ed-Dimiryaht stepped
To Azraeel, and from him received the Sword,   700
Aud cast himself again into the gulf
That yawned beneath him, and with lightning speed,
He rushed through every world, until he stood
Within the Hall of Iblees, where he mixed
Unnoticed with the crowd of Chiefs who stood   705
In reverence round the son of Jarjarees.

CANTO III.

THE COUNCIL OF KINGS.

EL HAHRITH from his throne at length arose,
And all was silence, and his voice alone
In that wide hall was heard, as thus he spoke:
"Kings of the Jinn, the son of Jarjarees   710
Before you stands; my elder brethren fell
By Allah's minions murdered, in the fight
In which my father died. Remember ye
How mighty was the strength of Jarjarees,
And how he must have overcome his foes,   715
If some who meanly dreaded Allah's wrath,
And some who feared that Jarjarees would seize
The kingdoms which they ne'er deserved to rule,
Had not in fear or malice, kept aloof
Far from the din of war? On them be shame!   720
The power of Jarjarees was overthrown,
And since his death no king has ever dared
To war with Allah, or proclaim himself
The leader of the monarchs of the Jinn.
Kings, hither called by me, I bid you choose   725
A Chieftain who shall fill my father's throne,
And wage with Allah never-ceasing war.
Whom therefore should you choose beside myself,
The sole surviving son of Jarjarees?
My father's magic armour I possess, [25]   730
And you shall swear to aid me with your arms,
Till Allah and his servants perish all,
Or abdicate in fear their thrones of light,
And vainly seek to hide from us in Hell.

Take then the oath. My troops are all around,   735
And no one shall refuse, for am not I
The only hero who refused to stoop
Before a thing of earth which Allah made?
And think you with an army at my back,
That such as I will brook the insolence,   740
Of any monarch here who dares rebel
Against the son of mighty Jarjarees?
Kings of the Jinn, ye take the oath or die!"
    The Kings who served his father crowded round
And bent the knee before him, but the Kings   745
Who would not follow Jarjarees to war,
And those who never knew that rebel Chief,
Stood all irresolute; they did not dare
To war with Allah, yet the troops around
Stood waiting but the word to slay them all.   750
    Thus long had Ed-Dimiryaht silent stood,
But now he stepped among the wavering kings,
And thus addressed them: "Princes, do not fear
The threats of Iblees. I am sent from Heaven
To save you from his vengeance, and I grasp   755
The sword of Azraeel."
                Then he forced his way
Among the amazed and unresisting guards,
Until he stood before the throne, where sat
The rebel Iblees, when again he spoke:
"El Hahrith, though your soul is black with sin,   760
Yet Allah's pardon waits you if you come,
And yield to him in peace. Reflect awhile.
Almighty is the King whom once you served,
And how shall you oppose him? Know you not,
That had the righteous monarchs of the Jinn   765

Declared themselves allies of Jarjarees,
Yet Allah's forces must have conquered all?
You may indeed maintain your ground awhile,
Though struggling blindly in the hand of God,
For he may wisely let you rule awhile, 770
That greater good from evil may result.
But fear you not the Trumpet? Fear you not
The Sword of Azraeel?"
      Iblees heard, and sat
A moment silent, while a smile of scorn
Flashed like the lurid lightning o'er his face: 775
"I reck not what befalls", at length he cried,
"For Allah is my mortal enemy.
But lo, before you, monarchs of the Jinn,
You see a greater God than Allah's self,
In me. O Ed-Dimiryaht, dare you come 780
To counsel me to stoop before a King
Whom I despise? But you shall see my power,
For I have here a prisoner who has lain
In chains to wait my wrath. Prepare yourselves,
O ye rebellious Kings, to yield or die. 785
Go, bring Marjahneh hither!"
       Thus he spoke,
And Ed-Dimiryaht deigned not to reply:
But round him thronged the Kings who would not stoop
To Iblees, and with no divided voice,
Proclaimed him King of the Believing Jinn. 790
The troops of Iblees every sword unsheathed,
Expecting his command to hew them down,
When harsh the clanking of a chain was heard,
And calm and self-collected even then,
Marjahneh stood before them. On her brow 795

They saw a streak of fire, where jagged rocks
Had touched her, and her hair disordered hung
Around her, and her plumes were crushed and bruised
By the great weight of stone. Then Dahsim rose,
And turning to his daughter he exclaimed: 800
"Jinnceyeh, will you yield to Iblees now?
If Allah could protect his wretched slaves,
You perhaps might hope assistance at his hands:
Lo, every monarch af the Jinn has sworn
To yield to Iblees, and shall you refuse?   805
Has insufficient punishment been yours,
Or will you still provoke us till we rise,
And slay you as an enemy of all
Who bow before the son of Jarjarees?"
    "Think not", she answered, "that I am alone.   810
Though all the monarchs of the Jinn rebel
Against the might of Allah, he is here
To strengthen me to meet whate'er befalls."
She looked around her and perceived the Kings
Who stood by Ed-Dimiryaht. "Kings, behold   815
How Iblees, tyrant as he is, can treat
Those who defy his power! O trust not him!
Dahsim, behold the Kings who will not yield
To Iblees! See, I do not stand alone,
For these are not his slaves, and in the midst   820
Stands Ed-Dimiryaht, who has never stooped
To any King but Allah!"
                        While she spoke,
A wrathful murmur rose among the Kings,
And every sword was drawn and tightly grasped
Although they wished not to commence the fight,   825
Till Iblees forced it ou them in his ire.

Then Iblees spoke. "Bring here the magic arms
Of Jarjarees, and soon the Kings shall own
His son's resistless might. I'll slay them all,
And wrest the Sword of Azraeel from the grasp   830
Of Ed-Dimiryaht, who alone has dared
To rouse the rebels to resist their King."
In haste he donned the arms, and raised his spear,
When Ed-Dimiryaht bade the Kings retire,
And leave him singlehanded to oppose   835
His fearful foe. The way was scarcely clear,
When Iblees rushed against him. Up he raised
The Sword of Azraeel sheathed, and with the sheath
He smote his enemy. The clashing arms
Fell before Ed-Dimiryaht. Iblees fled   840
In terror and confusion to his throne:
When Ed-Dimiryaht took the enchanted arms,
And in the sight of Iblees girt them on.
    While Iblees sat confounded, Dahsim felt
An anger by reflection uncontrolled,   845
And with the anger of a baffled Chief
Who wreaks his bootless rage on all around,
He turned upon Marjahneh in his wrath,
And cried in furious accents, "Will you yield
To Iblees now? Reflect upon your doom.   850
The upper worlds are beautiful and bright,
But this an awful chaos. You shall pine
For ever in our dungeons hopelessly,
For if you will not yield to Iblees now,
I'll break your wings, and chain you in a cave."   855
Bright was the light that flashed-amid the hall,
For all the foes of Iblees clothed their forms
In wreaths of flame, prepared for utmost strife.

Speechless with anger Ed-Dimiryaht stood
A moment, then he drew a flaming sword   860
Steeped in the burning drops of gall which cause
Death, paleness, putrefaction. On he sprang,
And lifting up his blade in act to strike,
He held the fearful sword o'er Dahsim's head,
And cried, "O Dahsim, speak another word.   865
And over you I shed the dews of death,
And the Siraht would sink beneath your weight."
Dahsim recoiled in terror, while the chains
Marjahneh wore, fell clanking to the ground,
And she was freed, and Ed-Dimiryaht turned,   870
And led her to the Kings. O mournfully
Her answer to her father smote the ear!
    "O woe to me, for fatherless am I!
The tyranny of those who league themselves
Against the might of Allah, never yet   875
Devised a greater punishment than this.
To me, your daughter, you employed the threat,
And I renounce you till the day when God
Shall lead you from your sins. Alas, alas,
Before the fall of Iblees, who would think   880
That I could thus address you! Though I live
Until the Trumpet's Second Blast resounds,
I never can forget that you were once
My father, but unworthy as you are,
I call you so no longer. All is changed.   885
O Dahsim, I would gladly die for you,
And would not grudge life, liberty, or wings,
If you from your apostacy would turn.
We once were friends in Heaven, but never more
We meet in love again. Alas for me,   890

For truly worse than fatherless am I!"
Her voice was lost in sobs; when Iblees rose,
And called his sons around him and prepared
To rush against his enemies. They charged,
When Ed-Dimiryaht raised the Archangel's sword   895
And waved it round his head. His foes fell back,
Senseless as though a shooting star had struck
Their frames of fire.[26]   He called the faithful Kings:
"Quit, quit for ever this accursed world!
The highest Earth is like a lower Heaven;   900
And we will found a mighty empire there
And call it inneestahn.[27] Abandon now
Their palace to the wicked."
                              Then he sprang
Swift from the hall, attended by his troops,
Nor did they set their feet upon the ground,   905
Till they alighted on the highest Earth.

CANTO IV.

THE GIFTS OF AZRAEEL.

LET no vain mortal seek the mountain Kahf,
The mountain which surrounds the highest Earth!
The fleetest horseman scarce could cross the world
From Kahf to Kahf, although five hundred years   910
He spent upon the journey. He would pass
All habitable regions, and beyond
Would trackless deserts, full of monstrous beasts,
Impede his progress, and although he passed

Unhurt, the thousand perils of the way,   915
And though he lived to reach the Outer Sea,
The Circumambient Ocean, where it flows
Between the earth and Kahf, yet still the sea,
Would bar him from his goal. Tremendous storms,
And fishes that could gulp a mountain down, [28]   920
Protect the Emerald Mountain where it rears
Its mighty peaks, two thousand miles in height,
Above the stormy sea. So has it stood
Since first the earth was peopled with the Jinn,
And so the mountain evermore shall stand,   925
Nor shall it crumble when Israhfeel sounds
The Blast of Consternation.
                                Brightly shone
The sun upon the emerald heights of Kahf,
And Ed-Dimiryaht and his friends resolved
To form their dwelling near it. Soon they found   930
A lovely Alpine valley. Lofty hills
Closed it on every side except the West,
Where the great Ocean rolled its stormy waves.
    Then Ed-Dimiryaht thus addressed the Kings:
"Here, chieftains, will we dwell. The highest Earth 935
Presents no spot so fit for our abode.
The Diving Jinn beneath this sea may plunge,   .
And we will rear our cities ou the land.
Assemble all your subjects, nor delay,
But build a glorious home, twixt earth and air.   940
First, to protect the kingdom from the sea,
Form ye a Coral Reef, whereon the waves
May break in powerless wrath."
                                The Kings obeyed,
And sought their separate kingdoms, whence they called

Their subjects, and commanded them to join   945
The King of the Believing Jinn, and act
Obedient to his orders. All the Kings
Departed on their errand, and alone
Were Ed-Dimiryaht and Marjahneh left.
    Marjahneh weeping sat upon a rock,   950
Heartbroken at the loss of all her friends,
And in the weakness of despairing grief
At times regretted, half unconsciously,
(Now that the fury of the strife was o'er,
Wearied with grief, she rather felt than thought)   955
She had not deigned to yield, and tamely crouch
Before the rebel Iblees. "Woe to me,
For I shall ne'er behold my father more",
She cried, "my mother and my brethren too,
Have yielded to their King, but who am I,   960
Who rashly dared oppose him?"
                       As she spoke,
A murmur sweeter than Israhfeel's voice,
Thrilled through her heart, — the voice of God himself!
    "O weep for those who yielded to the Fiend;
But now the strife is o'er, the victory won,   965
Regret not thou the firmness of thy soul!
The Scemurgh[29] sits to all eternity,
For ever lonely on the heights of Kahf,
And views with eyes that never move or sleep,
The countless changes of the universe.   970
But dost thou think the bird regrets her fate,
And views with envy happier, meaner birds;
Or dost thou think the sleepless guardian sits
Contented with the awful charge that God
Assigned her? O Marjahneh, not for thee,   975

Has God decreed the Seemurgh's awful lot,
But happier cares, though meaner, shall be thine:
Trust thou in God, and all shall yet be well!"
  She heard, and she was calmed, and inly prayed;
"O God, restore me to my friends again,   980
And let me dwell where'er their lot is cast:
But, O my Father, not for Heaven itself
Would I renounce thy holy voice within,
Which tells me thou hast smiled upon thy child!"
  Then Ed-Dimiryaht spoke. "We may not weep 985
Our former friends. We must not fear for them.
Though the Siraht should sink beneath their feet,
They are not lost for ever. God is good,
And 'tis the foulest slander on his name,
To think, as Iblees shall persuade mankind,   990
That he, the Just, the Merciful, will hurl
To torments that shall never have an end,
The fools who dare oppose him! You alone
Of Iblees' race accursed, dared to stand
Beside the King of the Believing Jinn.   995
Of all our race, we only own the might
Of Allah. You alone remained my friend,
Throughout our fearful struggle. Do not weep,
For we may suffer, though we must not sin,
If we to God are faithful. O my God,   1000
I thank thee, thou hast given the strength to two
Of Iblees' house accursed, to resist
His evil counsels! Not for twenty worlds,
Would I be now as Iblees! Praised be God,
That two survive the fall of Iblees' house!   1005
Marjahneh, I have loved you since the time
When we were children in the groves of Heaven,

And chased our playmates through the densest shades,
Or danced upon the boughs which could not break,
But swayed beneath us as instinct with life;   1010
And Heaven grew brighter hour by hour to see
The joy of those amid its glory born.
Lonely art thou, Marjahneh; lonely I;
But share with me the Throne of Jinneestahn,
And I will love you next to God himself."   1015
    She took his hand and answered, "Be it so!
Beside you none could fitly claim my love.
You snatched me from my foes, and evermore
I pledge myself to you. May God approve!"
    They knelt upon the gleaming rocks of Kahf,   1020
And sanctified the compact by a prayer.
"O Father, thou hast saved us from our foes:
O sanctify our union; give us back
Our enemies as friends, and bless the Kings
Who yielded not to Iblees, but to earth   1025
Have come with us, obedient to thy will.
Have mercy on, and bless us, O our God!"
    Their short and humble prayer was quickly o'er,
And when they rose, they far away perceived
A solemn rushing sound. "We hear the wings   1030
Of Azraeel," Ed-Dimiryaht then exclaimed.
"He doubtless comes for this tremendous Sword,
And though the wicked dread him as a foe,
Yet has he been a friend indeed to us."
Marjahneh fixed her eyes upon the ground,   1035
But Ed-Dimiryaht met the Archangel's glance
Unshrinking. Azraeel soon before them stood,
And in his usual solemn tones he spoke.
    "With prudent wisdom have you used the Sword,

But now restore it to the hands that lent.   1040
The magic arms of Jarjarees are yours,
And nought can foil the spells of Jarjarees,
Except the eternal Name of God himself,
Which Iblees neither can nor dare employ
Against you, though in ages yet to come,   1045
A son of Adam o'er the earth shall rule,
To whom a Seal is granted, with the Name
Of God engraved upon it. All your race
Must serve this King, for none shall e'er oppose
His awful power, and live. The Seal he wears   1050
A crafty Efreet shall contrive to steal,
And lead the armies of rebellious Jinn
Against you, but resist them to the last,
And I will save you ere your empire falls.
Iblees will ne'er assail you after that,   1055
But he will strive to conquer Jinneestahn
Unceasingly before this last repulse,
And you must be for ever on your guard.
Well have you both opposed his ill designs!"
      Before him Ed-Dimiryaht humbly bowed,   1060
And in his hand he placed the Sword of Death.
Then Azraeel spoke again: "On all thy land,
On thee and all thy subjects be the grace
And favour of the only God you serve!
God's blessing be on thee above the rest,   1065
O Ed-Dimiryaht; and on thee beside,
Marjahneh, lovely Queen of Jinneestahn!
In token of God's favour, see the power
The Sword of Death conceals!"

                            He spoke, and shook
The Sword around him, and the barren rocks   1070

Were covered with the brightest flowers of Heaven.
Then Azraeel dipped his sword-blade in the sea:
"Behold the City of the Diving Jinn!"
He spoke, and lo, the waves recede for miles,
And in the distance instantly arose   1075
A Coral Reef, and nearer to the shore,
Appeared the City of the Diving Jinn,
Of amber wholly formed, and Amberabahd [30]
Thus most deservedly named. The waters rolled
Back o'er the lovely city, but they lay   1080
Calm as a lake, and scarce a ripple broke
The shining ocean. Those eternal storms
Which o'er the Outer Ocean ever sweep,
Upon the Coral Reef expend their force.
   Then Azraeel smote his sword upon the earth, 1085
And while ten thousand, thousand lightnings flash,
Arose in all its splendour on their sight,
Joharahbahd, the pride of Jinneestahn,
A city wholly built of precious gems.
   "Lo, such the glories God assigns to you",   1090
Said Azraeel, "but his bounty does not end
With even gifts like these. Behold again!"
   Above the city countless rainbows arched, [31]
Surpassing in intensity of light,
Full many a glory in the Heavens themselves,   1095
And round the city twined unnumbered fires,
Of every brilliant colour. Next arose
A red, a green, a white, a yellow sun,
A fifth was blue, while many a moon arose,
Each larger than the moon that shines on earth,   1100
And six huge arches formed of mingled moons.
Huge trees, so vast that e'en the smallest spray

Would seem an Adansonia, grew around,
O'erhung with loveliest flowers of every hue.
The twining flames that round the city coiled, 1105
Seemed now like tropic creepers, now they seemed
Like monstrous serpents. Changing thus, behold
White lights, and blue, and red, and purple shone,
Veering and shifting, while beneath the light
Of these enchanted splendours which surpass 1110
All else in brilliancy, the city shines
Yet brighter every moment, and the stones,
Sparkle and glitter ceaselessly. There reigns
Eternal summer, heavy clouds are none,
The wind blows not, nor falls the rain or dew, 1115
Unwatered and unsown, the country yields
A harvest of the brightest flowers and fruits;
And neither beast nor bird nor insect dares
To harm the fairy realms of Jinneestahn,
Though to its splendours not to be conceived, 1120
They add their thousand beauties. But to see
The glory of the country as it is,
Above the highest rainbows fly the Jinn,
And gaze upon the splendours far below.
This is the grandest sight in Jinneestahn! 1125
    Like three huge pairs of wings expanded wide,
Behold the Jewel City's triple walls,
Of diamond, to protect it when besieged.
Yet even these must fall before the Seal,
Nor shall the city ever need them more. 1130
    On splendours hardly known in Heaven itself,
Did Ed-Dimiryaht and Marjahneh gaze
Bewildered for a time, and when they turned,
They found themselves alone. His work was done,

And Azraeel had not stayed to hear their thanks. 1135
They rose amid the splendours to survey
The unequalled glories of Joharahbahd,
Their gorgeous dwelling. Soon the Kings returned,
And led their subjects with them, and they gazed
Amazed upon the flaming lights around. 1140
 "All you behold," King Ed-Dimiryaht cried,
"Is the free gift of God. Let none regret
The gloomy realms of Iblees. In the West,
You see the Coral Reef. Let guards be placed
To watch the boundary line of Jinneestahn, 1145
Aud warn us when our vengeful enemies
Approach. To you, King Sahleb, ³² I assign
The ocean as your kingdom. You alone
Of all the Diving Kings have joined my bands,
And justly are you ruler of the sea. 1150
A city is already reared for you,
And though it does not shine as bright as mine,
Yet is it lovely. It is as the moon:
Joharahbahd resembles more the sun."
 King Sahleh, when he heard the monarch's words, 1155
Plunged with his followers in the placid sea.
The Divers love their beauteous city well,
Nor are they envious of a brighter sphere.
A beauty, softer than Joharahbahd's,
Prevails in Amberabahd eternally. 1160
 Long ages passed in happiness and peace,
Ere Iblees, who had fixed his earthly throne
In Western Kahf, ³³ could find his enemies.
Yet ever they opposed him when he strove
To wreak his wrath on man. The Evil Jinn 1165
Had lost their innocence and endless youth.

Their souls that knew no peace, unceasingly
Weakened their powers. Their evil cunning grew,
And still increased; all other powers of mind
Were more or less destroyed; and evermore,   1170
Their plagues and outward signs of woe increased.
Thus could they not perceive their enemies,
Who strove to bring to nought their evil schemes:
But when they once discovered Jinneestahn,
They long maintained a constant border-war,   1175
Attempting vainly to subdue their foes,
Or pass the Coral Reef that barred the way.

END OF THE FIRST BOOK.

BOOK THE SECOND.

MEYMOONEH.

ARGUMENT.

I. Birth and education of Ed-Dimiryaht's daughter, Meymooneh. Ed-Dimiryaht sends her to the earth to oppose the troops of Iblees. Her flight across the Circumambient Ocean. Her journey to Siberia. The Teutons. Meymooneh's contest with an Efreet. Her conversation with Thora.

II. Meymooneh pursues the Efreet to the Throne of Iblees in Western Kahf. Repentance of Zelemboor. Meymooneh sends a detachment of Ed-Dimiryaht's troops to guard Siberia. She leads Zelemboor to Ed-Dimiryaht's palace, and then lies down to rest among the splendours over the City of Jewels. Jebraeel appears to her. Ed-Dimiryaht departs to Jerusalem.

CANTO I.

JINNEESTAHN AND SIBERIA.

THERE was rejoicing at Joharahbahd,
And Ed-Dimiryaht and Marjahneh less
Lamented their unworthy friends, who dared
Resist their God; for God to them has sent

A daughter; and the Queen Marjahneh said,　　　　5
"Call her Meymooneh, [34] call her Fortunate!"
　They taught Meymooneh all their powerful spells,
And how to fight with fire, and how to move
Revealed to other beings; and how concealed
From human eyes and evil Jinn remain.　　　　10
But when she asked to view the World of Men,
King Ed-Dimiryaht answered, "Risk it not
Till I permit you; for our deadliest foes
Are ever working evil in the world,
And therefore Earth is not as Jinneestahn.　　　　15
A huge blue vault o'erspreads the World of Men,
A sun, a moon, and stars alone adorn
The day and night, and often heavy clouds
Veil these from men. Their eyes could never bear
The darkest night that reigns in Jinneestahn.　　　　20
Before, Meymooneh, we can think you fit
To stand among us other than a child,
Alone amid our deadliest enemies
I'll send you forth to range the human world,
And thwart their schemes for causing sin and woe!"　25
　Thus Ed-Dimiryaht answered her whene'er
The Princess asked to journey to the earth.
Then would she seek the Coral Reef, and gaze
Upon the stormy sea beyond, with dread
And wonder, or would watch the guards who paced　30
Along the reef, or soared into the air
To scan the distance for a hostile wing.
Then would Meymooneh plunge amid the waves
Within the reef, and seek the ocean bed
To view the city Amberabahd; then rise,　　　　35
And hover in the splendours that o'erhang

Joharahbahd, and let the mingled rays,
(Rivers of glory 'twixt the earth and heaven,
Flowing in oceans, not in rays, of light,
From heaven to earth, and back from earth to heaven, 40
Commingling in ten thousand various hues);
Play o'er her sparkling feathers; and behold
The coloured suns, as one by one they sank
Behind the peaks of Kahf; and see the moons
And shining belts display their silver light.   45
   O, beautiful is night in Jinneestahn!
For high above its cities shine the moons,
And the huge moon-like belts, the rainbows shine
With softened lustre, and the countless gems
Glitter and flash with hues that never day   50
Elicits from them, while the ghostly gleam
Of the expanded diamond domes has power
To throw an awe on those who know the sign,
Aud realise a future dreadful war,
In which Joharahbahd shall be besieged,   55
And not the strongest talisman shall save
The wearer, who shall mingle in the fight
With those who bear with them Suleymahn's Seal!
   At length she learned the wisdom of her race,
When Ed-Dimiryaht thought that it was right   60
To let the Princess see the World of Men.
He sent for Queen Marjahneh, and began:
"Meymooneh must not always here remain,
But westwards she must bend her flight alone,
And strive against the suffering and the sin   65
That weighs the sons of Adam to the ground."
   "Alone!" Marjahneh answered, "dare you trust
Your daughter 'mid the hosts of fiends that range

The world, alone? O, do not risk so much!
Why should she ever leave our land of light,   70
Or wherefore should she leave without a guard?"
   He heard, and he replied in firmer tones,
Though tinged with sadness, that convinced the Queen
She could not hope to bend him from his word,
And that he acted as he thought was right,   75
Yet sore against his will, "O, tempt me not!
Remember, 'tis the law of Jinneestahn,
That all our children thus must range the world,
Ere they can be our equals. Ask me not,
Although the King, to violate the law,   80
And introduce dissension, thus to play
Into the hands of Iblees! Though I feared
More for the safety of my child than you,
Yet would I send her forth into the world!
She has learned all that she can learn from us,   85
But not experience, which, like Adam's race,
We gain not save by danger or by sin!
I fear not for Meymooneh: she is clothed
In spotless innocence, and thus might dare
To trust herself alone among the hosts   90
Of Iblees, in the gloomy West of Kahf.
But there I will not send her. She may go
And range about the world, and if she seeks
The realms of Iblees of her own accord,
Confiding in her own inherent power   95
Of virtue, she will thence escape unharmed:
But if I sent her thither, I should feel
As if I wantonly were tempting God!"
   Marjahneh did not answer him at once:
She turned away awhile, and hid her face,   100

And shuddered, then she raised again her head,
And resolutely faced him, and drew up
Her figure proudly to its utmost height.
    "What! should the Queen of Jinneestahn oppose
The customs of the country! Think it not!   105
I yield! Meymooneh shall depart alone,
Amid the thousand perils of the earth,
If she herself should wish it."
                              Then she took
A packet of her daughter's hair, [35] and cast
A portion in a fire, and as it burned,   110
Slow gliding through the roof of solid stone [36]
That could not bar the way, Meymooneh came,
And noiselessly, with open wings, she slid
Down to the palace floor.
                         "You called me here,
And I obey the summons," she exclaimed: 115
"Wherever you may send me, will I go,
Though you should bid me venture to the Throne
Of Iblees on the accursed Seventh Earth."
    "Nay," Ed-Dimiryaht answered, "risk not this:
But you must seek the earth, and strive alone   120
Against the might of Iblees. Do not fear,
And God will guard you, though you fight in vain,
As it may seem to you, with countless foes,
And all your friends are far beyond your reach."
    "Yes", cried Meymooneh, "I have long desired   125
To view the World of Men. I only ask
One favour from you. If I should return
With honour from this present enterprise,
Then grant that when Joharahbahd's besieged,
I may not stand inactive, but may fight   130

Among the foremost who defend the town."
"Go on your mission now," replied the Queen;
"Too proud are the Jinneeyehs to refrain
From fighting with the overwhelming hosts,
When strongest walls shall yield before a Seal   135
That holds the Jinn in service. Go your way,
And may that God we worship guide your path!"
    Meymooneh stayed no longer; her desire
Was given her now, and joyfully she flew
Westwards, until she lighted on the reef   140
That holds the stormy Outer Sea at bay.
Awhile she stood, and gazed on Jinneestahn;
Then to the sea she turned, and up she sprang,
And plunged amid the darkness and the storm.
    Loud was the thunder of the waves that dashed   145
Their waters on the reef, and black as ink,
The rolling billows seemed, o'ertopped with weeds,
And heaped from base to crest with muddy foam.
Fierce hurricanes rushed forth on every side;
The wind each moment changed to urge them on;   150
From every quarter came the heaviest rain,
Thick as a mighty cataract that falls
In torrents from a mountain's rugged sides.
The tossing billows met the driving clouds
Which almost rested on the sea, yet rose   155
Thick as the smoke of Hell, aloft in air,
Too high for sight. Meymooneh could not rise
Above the clouds, for she could scarcely fly
Above the water, or avoid the waves,
So heavy with the water were her wings.   160
And even if she shook or burned them dry,
The water rushed upon her instantly,

And made her flight yet heavier than before.
Still on she struggled, though she could not see
The shore she strove to reach, the sky above,   165
Nor yet the land she left; she only saw
The waves that foamed so fearfully below.
At length she sank amid the waves, but rose,
And shook the water off as best she might,
And fought unconquered with the wind and rain.   170
   Meymooneh could not see the distant land,
But, 'mid the roaring of the storm, she heard,
The waves that broke upon an earthly shore.
At length she felt the hurricane had ceased,
And she had reached the deserts that surround   175
The World of Men on every side. She fell
Senseless, with wings expanded, on the sand,
Exhausted by her struggle with the storm.
   The Outer Ocean is a fearful flight
To those who first attempt to cross its waves;   180
But when they once have passed it, it presents
No further terrors to them, for they learn
To fly above the storms.
                 Meymooneh lay
Conscious of nought but weariness and strife,
Too weary either to repose or sleep   185
Until the sun revived her. She arose,
And looked with wonder on the scene around.
She stood amid a desert, where there grew
No tree or shrub, as far as eye could reach
'Twas one vast plain of dingy sand. She heard   190
The distant roaring of the Outer Sea,
Behind her.
       "Strange and wonderful is this!"

She cried, "alone I wander in the world,
Amid the perils of the Outer Sea,
And through the pathless deserts. Am not I,　　195
The Princess of the Jinn? Yet here I stand
All unattended, and I cannot guess
What future dangers wait me on my flight.
King Ed-Dimiryaht's daughter shall not shrink
From peril or from suffering! I behold　　　200
The huge blue vault of which my father spoke,
And one pale sun. O how unlike is this
To all the splendours of Joharahbahd!
But here I cannot stay, for I must fly
Far westward, till I reach the homes of men."　205
　　She spoke and sprang again into the air,
And left the Outer Ocean far behind.
The shifting sands she passed, the earth grew green,
And all around her lay the World of Men,
Adorned with woods and mountains and with streams, 210
And oceans, and with meadows. On she flew
Above the varied country, till she saw
Amid the frozen deserts of the North,
The parents of the mighty Teuton race,
Who wandered northwards from a milder clime　215
And strengthened there their offspring to become
The universal monarchs of the seas,
And overthrow all tyrannies, and light
The torch of freedom for the modern world.
There dwelt the early Teutons, on the coast,　　220
Rugged and blocked with icebergs as it is,
That forms the Asian boundary on the North.
There, where primeval forests grew and died,
Through which the mammoth and the mastodon

Went crashing their unwieldy limbs, in vain   225
Seeking escape from hunters, whom they taught
Never to quail before an earthly foe,
And ne'er to yield, not e'en when overcome. [37]
　Meymooneh watched the hunters, and she knew
The future leaders of the world were there;   230
Then to their villages she turned, and saw
A crowd who stood around an aged Chief,
Whose giant limbs proclaimed enormous strength,
Though he was old and feeble, and could hope
No more to wield the weapons of his youth.   235
He sat, relating to his younger friends,
The dangers he had braved. Meymooneh mixed
Unseen among the hearers, and perceived,
At every word the aged Chieftain spoke,
How eagerly the crowd around him heard.   240
The youths were waving spears and arrows high,
Or proudly felt their points. The girls stood near,
And trembled at the dangers he had braved,
And yet escaped unhurt. But now, behold,
An evil Jinnee mingles with the throng,   245
And whispers venomed counsels in their ears.
　"Why", cried the Chieftain, "should our heroes toil
To win a hard subsistence from the hunt,
When prosperous nations further to the south,
Are ripe for plunder? Thither let us march,   250
And wrest the country from the hands of those
Who could not by their valour hold their own.
What save the toil and danger can we gain
By mammoth-hunts? March therefore on the South,
And plunder all you meet."
　　　　　　　　　With cries of joy,   255

4

The fiercer youths received the old man's words:
But one fair girl came forward, and she fell
Before the Chief, scarce knowing what she said,
Although Meymooneh's power had given her words.
"Nay, know you not that luxury unnerves   260
The nations of the South, that you would fain
Meet in unequal contest? True it is,
The stalwart warriors of the North would crush
The puny South to dust beneath their feet;
But are they not unworthy of our arms,   265
And would not every snare that weakens them,
Destroy our power? More worthy enemies
Than the degenerate children of the South,
Roam wild among the forests."
                         Those who heard,
Gathered in groups, disputing. But the Chief   270
Motioned for silence, and commenced again:
  "Well spoken, Thora![38] Yes, the Southern tribes
Are all unworthy of a Northman's arms;
So leave them to their luxury and sloth,
Till they at length give place to better men.   275
'Twere cowardice to fall upon them now,
And cowardice and cruelty exist
In Northern bosoms never; they remain
Among the curses of the Southern tribes.
Depart ye therefore, but direct your arms   280
Against the mammoth, not against the South."
  The Efreet mingled with the listening throng,
And while he tried to rouse them to the war,
Meymooneh, visible to him alone,
Addressed him: "Wherefore should you rouse a war 285
That cannot but destroy the innocent,

And surely cannot lead to good, as yet?"
He answered fiercely, "Wherefore have you come
To interfere with those to whom is given
The race of man by Allah? Are not we   290
The weapons of His vengeance on mankind?"
  He spoke, and turned away. Meymooneh strove
Against him in the souls of those who spoke
In favour of the hunt and not the war.
At length she conquered, and the Efreet fled   295
Baffled before her. Then the crowd dispersed,
And Thora stayed alone. Meymooneh took
A human form. "Whence, maiden, had you power",
She asked, "to move the Chieftain to reflect
Again upon the war? The Southern tribes   300
Have not the truth or justice, or the strength,
That ever mark the children of the North,
Although they far surpass them in their arts.
A time shall come when Northern arms shall crush
The South before them, and shall learn their arts   305
From those that they have conquered, yet retain
The prowess of the North; — but not for years."
  The girl replied, "You saw the aged Chief?
My father and my mother both are dead:
His daughter was my mother, and he clings   310
To me as to his last support in life.
But whence are you? for all the country near,
And all its tribes I know, but ne'er have seen
Your face before, and trackless forests stretch
For miles and miles along this frozen coast."   315
  Meymooneh heard, and with a smile replied,
"My country, Jinneestahn, is far away.
Its princess am I, but I roam alone

About this gloomy earth, where dwell the sons
Of Adam. Far I journeyed from the East,   320
And when I saw the concourse round the Chief,
I stopped to learn the cause."
                    'Tis stranger still,"
Said Thora, speaking partly to herself,
"Of all the nations of the earth, I know
Not one that calls its country Jinneestahn   325
Stranger, no Northern princess can you be:
If Southern, wherefore thus despise the South:
And who can track the forests East and West!"
Then speaking louder, she exclaimed, "You come
Far from the East, you say. Is Jinneestahn   330
A brighter land than this? Our frozen coast
I hear, is far more gloomy than the South.
How gladly would I seek those Southern climes
Where frost and snow exist not! Yet I fear
Our Northern race would never deign to dwell   335
Among a Southern nation, and permit
That nation to retain their land in peace."
    Meymooneh answered, "See you not the Sun
That high above us stands? Your Northern Land
Rejoices in its summer now. Look up,   340
And fix your eyes unshrinking on the Sun!
Endure its light you cannot! We have five
That circle over us in Jinneestahn,
And other splendours more than I could name.
I'd gladly, when I fly to Jinneestahn, 39   345
Amid its splendours take you, but I know
No human strength of eye could bear the light.
You cannot even face your Northern Sun,
And how should you unblinded gaze around

Amid the thousand lights of Jinneestahn?"   350
"Are you not then a woman?" Thora cried,
Trembling with fear. "I pray you harm me not;
How can I face you fearlessly?"
                 She spoke, —
And straight the Princess her disguise threw off.
"Behold me in my glory", she exclaimed.   355
"Lo, I am a Jinneeyeh, as you see,
And daughter of the King of Jinneestahn."
Then Thora fell upon her knees dismayed:
She saw the Princess through a mist of flame, [40]
In her unearthly beauty, with a wreath   360
Of heavenly flowers twined round her radiant head,
And her great wings expanded, dazzling white,
So brilliant that against them snow would change
Blacker than coal from envy, as we see
A lime-ball black upon the Sun's bright disk! [41]   365
The bright Jinneeyeh stooped above the girl,
And spoke: "O Thora, thou who makest peace,
The peace of Heaven be on thee!"
                 Thora looked,
And lo, Meymooneh vanished as she came,
And Thora to her home returned in awe.   370

CANTO II.

MEYMOONEH AND ZELEMBOOR.

MEYMOONEH left Siberia far behind,
And hastened westwards, striving to o'ertake

The Efreet she had conquered, for she feared,
Lest he should rouse, before she tracked his flight,
His master's troops against the Teuton race,⁣   375
And lead them southward ere the appointed time.
She heeded not the countries which she passed,
Her eyes fixed ever on the distant sky.
At length she saw her foe, but well she knew
He could not see her, when she willed it not.   380
He never halted, or delayed his flight,
But closely by Meymooneh still pursued,
Swept o'er the western countries of the earth,
And o'er the pathless deserts. Still he flew
With unabated swiftness. Then he rose   385
Above the tempests of the Outer Sea,
Which howl with tenfold fury on the coasts
Where Iblees rears his throne upon the earth.
Well may the ocean bounding Western Kahf
Be called the Sea of Darkness, for it bounds   390
The regions where the Throne of Iblees stands,
When Iblees rises from the Seventh Earth!

   At length the Efreet reached the Throne, and cried,
"I cannot rouse the North against the South!
If we can do so, ere the empires shake,   395
Which, in the latter ages of the earth,
Shall be established in the world of men,
Then will the Teuton armies give themselves
To luxury and vice, and thus for years
Retard the plans of Allah."

                    "Is it so?"   400
El Aawar asked him, "have you been opposed?
On such a work as this must armies fly;
Myself shall head them, and with wine will drug

The Chieftains of that mighty Teuton race,
Which even now we view with shuddering fear."   405
   Then spoke Zelemboor, rising from his seat,
"Teer, Soht and Dahsim, on the Seventh Earth,
Are resting from their labours, wearied out
By striving with the foes we most detest.
They wait our orders; let us call them here,   410
And ere we act, confer with all our Chiefs."
   "So let it be, Zelemboor!" Iblees cried,
"And since to draw the Teutons into war
Would much advance our interests, I myself
Will call your brethren."
                Then he cleft the earth,   415
And down the gulf with lightning speed he plunged.
   Meymooneh watched Zelemboor, and perceived
He had not fallen so deeply as the fiends
Who stood around him; and his brother's face,
Had lost its heavenly beauty more than his;   420
And though a Chieftain of the Evil Jinn,
Some likeness to his son he still retained.
Meymooneh knew that he alone could see,
And he alone could hear her. She advanced,
And gently on his shoulder laid her hand.   425
"Zelemboor, son of Iblees, fear you not
The power of Allah, or does coward shame
Alone attach you to your father's cause?
Do you regret you feared to join your son,
Whom, save Marjahneh, none of Iblees' race   430
Have dared to join?"
             Zelemboor turned amazed,
And saw the Princess standing by his side.
Defiance was the feeling that arose

First in his heart, and fiercely he replied:
"Jinneeyeh, dare you Iblees' sons revile?   435
What matters it to you that I have joined
The army of the son of Jarjarees?
Who dares dispute the might of Jarjarees?
Was he not Allah's equal? Yet, alas,
My son defies the son of Jarjarees,   440
And rules a nation of rebellious Jinn,
Who will not stoop to Iblees."
                         Better thoughts
Rose in him at the mention of his son.
   "Woe to the race of Iblees! Woe to me!
Would I had joined my son! Our sinful deeds   445
I always hated! Would my son receive
His father, if he came repentantly,
To side with Allah? Who beside me stands?
Who of the daughters of Believing Jinn,
Has ventured here? O strange and wild the thought, 450
Yet even you yourself are like my son,
Although my countless sins obscure my sight,
And I behold you only as a mist,
And greater sinners see not even this."
   Then, turning to El Aawar, he exclaimed,   455
"Inform my father, when the council meets,
That some of my adherents on the earth
Require my instant presence."
                         He arose,
And left the council, and Meymooneh flew
Beside him o'er the gloomy Outer Sea: 460
And he continued, "You are yet a girl,
And of the daughters of Believing Jinn,
But few would venture to our gloomy realms.

I see you not save dimly through a mist,
But let me see you with the veil removed."   465
  She cast away the mist that veiled her form,
And in his wonderment he almost fell.
"You must", he cried, "indeed, indeed you must,
Be Ed-Dimiryaht's daughter! Lives he still,
And is the gorgeous world of Jinneestahn,   470
Bright as it seems, when we at times behold
Its flashing splendours from the Outer Sea?"
  "It is", the Princess answered, "as you say:
For Ed-Dimiryaht and Marjahneh live;
I am indeed their daughter, and I came   475
To view the realms of Iblees for myself,
Confiding in the invisibility
That hides us from the Unbelieving Jinn."
  As thus she spoke, a troop of Jinn approached,
Whom Ed-Dimiryaht stationed there to watch   480
The Sea of Darkness, and the leader bowed
Before Meymooneh.
                  "Princess, not for nought
Across this gloomy sea you dared to fly.
Whatever you command us, we obey
As if the King commanded."
                          She replied,   485
"Against the troops of Iblees guard the North,
Nor let them stir the Teutons up to war"
  Then said Zelemboor, "Let us join the Jinn,
And aid them guard Siberia. Should I go,
And strive to bend my father from his plans?"   490
  "Nay," said Meymooneh, "thither ne'er return.
My father's faithful servants will defend
Siberia from the hosts that Iblees leads.

Iblees would soon detect your altered mien,
And slay you. Rather would I fly with you,   495
To join our armies in the distant North,
But I am now o'erwearied, and the way
To Jinneestahn is long, so quit me not,
And I will lead you to the gorgeous realms
Where Ed-Dimiryaht rules. From thence I came 500
To fight my way across the sea, alone,
Before I called you forth from Western Kahf."

    Meymooneh led the way o'er many a land,
And many a fearful desert, till she reached
The Eastern Outer Ocean. High she rose   505
Above the clouds, and led Zelemboor on,
Until they reached the lovely blue lagoon,
That sleeps within the Reef of Jinneestahn.

    "Zelemboor", cried the Princess, "see you not
"The golden amber in the ocean depths?   510
It is a glorious city, Amberabahd,
With justice called the Moon of Jinneestahn.
Yet brighter splendours overspread the land,
Although the rainbows and the brilliant suns
Shine brightly on the ocean. Now behold   515
Joharahbahd, the Sun of Jinneestahn,
In all its glory! Notice how the stones
Change as the varied fires around them sweep,
And in the mingled rays of many a sun."

    Zelemboor speechless with surprise, beheld   520
The city blazing scarcely to be borne,
With suns and flames and rainbows. Down they sank
Amid its glories, and Meymooneh led
Zelemboor to the palace of the King,
Who strove by all his magic arts, to thwart   525

El Aawar's crafty, cruel scheme, to blind
The mighty Chieftains of the North with wine.
  He saw Zelemboor, and he ceased his spells.
"Thank God, Meymooneh, that I sent you not
To earth in vain, for you have hither led   530
My father, whom I never dared to hope
Would leave the troops of Iblees. Can it be,
O Father, that you now forsake your sins?
I would not willingly have caused you pain,
But dared not join the son of Jarjarees   535
In his insane rebellion."
                    As he spoke,
Zelemboor knelt before him, but he raised
His father up: "Zelemboor, do not stoop
To Iblees or to me, let Allah hear
Your prayers alone! I cannot speak the joy   540
I feel to see you here!"
                  Marjahneh came
To seek the King, and bade Meymooneh tell
The story of her journey. "You indeed
Are worthy of your station!" she exclaimed,
"And I proclaim you free from all restraints,   545
Save what the laws of God and Jinn impose.
Zelemboor from the realms of Iblees comes,
And I will join your father, and from him
Will learn how fare the Jinn that Iblees leads."
  As thus she spoke, Meymooneh left the hall,   550
And overwearied as she was, she flew
Among the highest rainbows, where she lay [42]
Resting amid the changing, shifting gleams
That played around her couch of brilliant light,
And gazing upward at the setting suns,   555

And hearing faintly angel songs in Heaven,
Till the bright light, and all the soothing sounds,
Lulled her to sleep. The moons and belts shone forth,
And bathed her in a sea of silver light,
Whose waves rolled silently around her couch,　　560
As she lay sleeping in her rainbow bed,
Without a dream of care, or thought of sin,
To dim the mirror of her perfect peace.
She thought not of the past, she needed not;
She thought not of the future; for she knew　　565
Her days were days of endless happiness,
Untouched by care or sin. She lay and slept
Till the red sun arose, and from its height
Flung down its roses o'er her. Up she sprang
And stood upon the rainbow, to behold　　570
The rising of the suns. The moving sea
Of vapours glowed beneath like scarlet wool,
And through it many a gorgeous hue appeared,
Born of the rosy light. Another sun
Arises, and its yellow rays descend,　　575
And alter all the landscape, and the peaks
Of Kahf are tinged with dazzling azure blue.
　　But vainly pen might strive to paint the scene
The Princess viewed. Familiar as she was
With every feature of that wondrous sky,　　580
Yet never did she feel its glory so,
As now, when absence for a single day
Had doubled all its charms. She stood and gazed,
A proud, triumphant feeling in her heart,
Like that we feel upon a starry night,　　585
And know not whence it comes. A murmured prayer
Of thankfulness and joy escaped her lips.

One glance alone had quenched an eagle's eye,
Had eagle stood beside her. Now behold,
A ray of glory falls, so dazzling white   590
That all the suns are darkened, and it shines
Around Meymoonch, and she sinks in awe
Down on her knees, and hides her dazzled eyes;
Yet, through her eyelids and her hands, the light
Seems to pervade her senses utterly.   595
    "Arise, beloved of God and angels, rise [43]
And hear the message sent thee from on high."
The Princess rose, and faced the painful light,
And saw the angel Jebracel by her side.
"Zclemboor ne'er shall join with lblees more,   600
But dwell with you, an equal and a friend.
In Heaven we honour you o'er all the troops
Of Ed-Dimiryaht, since to you belongs
The glory of Zelemboor's safe return
From Iblees' armies. To Jerusalem,   605
Let Ed-Dimiryaht, and his subject Kings
Depart, for there Suleymahn soon shall reign,
And he must be his Wezeer. When a fiend
Shall steal Suleymahn's Seal, he'll first command
That Iblees shall be worshipped. 'Tis the sign   610
By which King Ed-Dimiryaht, shall perceive
That he must lead his army to defend
Joharahbahd from Iblees. Peace to thee,
And to thy race, Meymooneh!"

                        As he spoke,
The suns shone forth from their eclipse of light,   615
And Jebraeel vanished; but the Princess flew
Swift to the city.

Ed-Dimiryaht sent
His messengers to call his subject Kings,
And left Joharahbahd, prepared to serve
As Wezeer, one to whom his mighty power   620
Was nothing, since all living things obeyed
The King Suleymahn, and his awful Seal.

END OF THE SECOND BOOK.

BOOK THE THIRD.

SULEYMAHN IBN DAHOOD.

ARGUMENT.

I. Suleymahn appoints Ahssaf and Ed-Dimiryaht his chief wezeers. His neglect of his prayers while inspecting some horses. His repentance and atonement. The Carpet of Suleymahn. Levy of his troops. Founding of the Temple. Punishment of a rebellious Efreet.

II. King Abd El Hahrith sends the Efreet Dahish to make a treaty with Suleymahn. Dahish stirs up his master to reject Suleymahn's terms. Great Battle between the Kings. Death of Abd El Hahrith. Imprisonment of Dahish.

III. The King of Sidon requests tribute of Suleymahn. The Power of Azraeel. Battle at Sidon. Death of the King, and destruction of the city. Narrow escape of Princess Jerahdeh.

IV. Suleymahn woos Jerahdeh. Her grief for her father. Dispute between Ed-Dimiryaht and Suleymahn. The Magic Statue. Idolatry of Jerahdeh. Faktash steals Suleymahn's Seal, and deposes him. Ed-Dimiryaht and his followers escape to Joharahbahd, placing Ahssaf in Amberabahd.

V. Ed-Dimiryaht marshals his troops. Jebraeel and Meymooneh. Faktash and Iblees lay siege to Joharahbahd. Battle between the walls of the city. Interposition of Azraeel. Azraeel drives Faktash from Suleymahn's throne. Faktash bound by Ed-Dimiryaht.

VI. Ahssaf wanders about in Amberabahd. Return of King
Sahleh. Their conversation. Ahssaf recalled to Jerusalem.

VII. The Galilean fisherman. Suleymahn recovers his Seal.
His return to Jerusalem. Faktash chained and thrown into the
Dead Sea. The Inhabitants of Sodom.

VIII. Suleymahn's pilgrimage to Mekkeh. He hears of Queen
Bilkees. He invites her to visit him at Jerusalem. Her throne and
her army. The gulf round Jerusalem. Meymooneh and Bilkees.
Suleymahn's reception of Bilkees. Their nuptials.

IX. Ahssaf's dream of the fall of Jerusalem. He calls Ed-
Dimiryaht. The Magic Mirror. Visions of the Future.

X. Old age of Suleymahn. His conversation with his wezeers.
Appearance of Jebraeel. His prophecies and consolations. Death
of Suleymahn. Death of Ahssaf, and return of Ed-Dimiryaht to Joharahbahd.

CANTO I.

THE SEAL AND THE CARPET.

In silent, anxious thought Suleymahn sat
Alone within his palace. "Who have I,"
He thought within himself, "that I can ask
To be my Wezeer of mankind? I wear
A Seal on which the Name of God is stamped,   5
And by its might all living things I rule.
What living man can rule the beasts and birds,
And how can I control the Evil Jinn?
Though God has placed their Chieftains in my power,
Confined by strongest chains, yet even I   10
View them with shuddering fear. My truest friend
Is Ahssaf [44], old Barkhiya's virtuous son:

Him will I make my Wezeer of mankind,
And he will teach me how to use my power,"
   Suleymahn clapped his hands; a servant came.   15
"Go, summon Ahssaf hither." He obeyed,
And Ahssaf shortly stood before the King.
"Ahssaf," Suleymahn cried, "behold my Seal!
All living things must serve it. Counsel me,
How I may best control the beasts and birds,   20
And more perplexing still than all beside,
Whom can I make my Wezeer of the Jinn?
I beg you as a friend, and as a King,
To serve me as my Wezeer of mankind."
   Ahssaf replied, "If you believe me fit,   25
No false humility shall make me shun
The arduous office."
           "On the Seal I wear,
Lay first your hand, and pledge yourself to act
With equal justice both to friends and foes;
And swear obedience to me on the Seal.   30
God deal with you as you shall deal with me!"
   Suleymahn spoke, and Ahssaf laid his hand
Upon the Seal, and took the solemn oath.
Then said the King again, "I do not know
How best to rule the beasts and birds and Jinn."   35
The hall was filled with Jinnees as he spoke,
And Ed-Dimiryaht thus addressed the King:
"Prophet of God, I come at His command,
To be your Wezeer, and to rule the Jinn.
I know the power inherent in your Seal,   40
And do not fear to pledge myself thereon.
The King of the Believing Jinn am I,
And Ed-Dimiryaht, King of Jinneestahn,

Will ne'er abuse his power, or dare to stoop
To Iblees and his servants."
                              "God be praised!"   45
Ahssaf exclaimed, "for he has surely sent
A messenger to rule for you the Jinn.
No Jinnee falsely swears upon the Seal!"
    Suleymahn sat unmoved, and gave his hand
To Ed-Dimiryaht, who upon the Seal,   50
And on the Name engraved upon the Seal,
Swore everlasting friendship with the King.
Suleymahn answered, "King of Jinneestahn,
God deal with you as you shall deal with me!
Among the Kings around you, have you none   55
Who under me will rule the beasts and birds?"
Two Jinnee Kings stepped forward, and they swore
To serve Suleymahn. "Do not now remain,"
Suleymahn answered, "but to-morrow lead
Your armies hither, for I wish to hold   60
A levy of my troops."
                              They bowed themselves
Before Suleymahn, and were gone. He looked
Around him, but beside him Ahssaf stood, —
Ahssaf alone, although the hall was filled,
When he dismissed the monarchs of the Jinn.   65
    Suleymahn said to Ahssaf, "View my troops.
To-morrow's levy must be such a scene,
As ne'er was witnessed in the world before.
The horses[45] which my father years ago
Took from the Amalekites, I now will see.   70
Give orders to the grooms to lead them out
Before me in the courtyard."
                              Ahssaf called

The grooms, and went to muster all his troops.
Suleymahn stood to view the steeds, and gazed
In admiration on them, and remained   75
Of all beside forgetful, till the shades
Of evening fell around him. "Woe to me!
May God forgive me!" then the King exclaimed:
"I have not offered up my noonday prayers,
Shame on me, that I thus neglect to praise   80
That God who gives me universal sway!"
He stood with knitted brow in mournful thought,
Then seized an axe that in the courtyard lay,
And as a sacrifice to God, the King
Nine hundred of the thousand horses slew.   85
At length an angel came, and stayed his hand.
"Prophet of God, your fault is well atoned,
And more than pardoned by the King of Heaven.
God gives you now dominion o'er the wind,
And sends a silken Carpet, green as grass,   90
Whereon your mighty armies all may stand,
And journey with the wind from place to place.
And yet it does not weigh a single pound, [46]
And you might roll it in a walnut shell,
Nor shall you ever find it large or small."   95
The angel vanished as Suleymahn took
The Carpet. "Just and righteous still thou art, .
O Allah!" he exclaimed, "and never more
Will I neglect the worship due to Thee.
To-morrow will I spread the Carpet out,   100
And there will orderly arrange my troops."
Thus speaking, to his palace he returned,
Revolving in his mind the strange events,
And checquered incidents that marked the day.

The morrow came at length, the King arose,   105
And led the troops without Jerusalem,
Then cast the Carpet down upon the ground,
And .it unrolled before him, till it spread
Far o'er the plain. Suleymahn placed his throne
Upon the Carpet. Ahssaf on the right   110
Sat with the human troops. The King stood up,
And let the sunlight sparkle on the Seal,
And called the Kings of the Believing Jinn.
"Lo", Ed-Dimiryaht answered, "all are here!"
And on Suleymahn's left the Jinnee stood,   115
His army round him, while in front of all,
An army marched of beasts; and overhead
The birds assembled, as a canopy
To shield Suleymahn's army from the sun.
"Behold!" Suleymahn cried, "I rule the wind,   120
And I command it to convey my troops
Above Jerusalem." The Carpet rose,
And slowly o'er the city's walls it sailed.
Suleymahn spoke. "My father wished to raise
A temple to the God we all adore.   125
This undertaking now devolves on me.
King Ed-Dimiryaht, bid the Jinn erect
A gorgeous temple on the hill below.
A stream of molten brass already flows
Where you must found the temple. But compel   130
The Evil Jinn to aid you in the work.
No human weakness is their unbelief,
But 'tis the sin inherent in the race
That counts all evil good."
                          The Carpet sank
Upon the hill below. The armies moved,   135

And stood around it, and Suleymahn bade
The Jinn remove his throne, and two obeyed.
Suleymahn seized the Carpet, when it rolled
Again into his hand. "Remove the troops
Of men, and beasts, and birds," he cried, "and ye, 140
Believing Jinn, prepare to rear a fane,
Of which Jerusalem shall long be proud!"
    Suleymahn still between his wezeers stood,
And he upraised the Seal, and by its might,
He bade the Evil Jinn that God had chained, 145
Appear; and aid King Ed-Dimiryaht's troops.
Huge heaps of metal and of stone were piled
Upon the hill. The Evil Jinn were forced,
Bound as they were, to lift the massive stones,
And lay them in the deep foundation pits. 150
Throughout the day the King and wezeers stood,
And saw them fix the stones, and make them firm,
With mortar from the spring of molten brass.
    At length the evening came. An Efreet stood,
And tried to spoil the work that he had done, 155
Unnoticed by his fellows. [47] He was seized,
And dragged before Suleymahn. "Bring me here
A brazen bottle", cried the angry King,
"And bring me here a cup of molten brass":
And these were placed before him as he spoke. 160
Suleymahn took the Seal, and stripped the chains
From off the Efreet. "In the name of God,
(The Name engraved upon this awful Seal)",
Suleymahn cried, "I bid you enter this."
The conquered Efreet grinned, and gnashed his teeth, 165
With rage and fear and hatred, but in vain.
Within the flask he crept, and then the King

Above him poured and sealed the molten brass.
"Beneath the sea for ages lie!" he cried,
"In mental suffering only, but so great,   170
That till the hand of man shall chance to break
The flask, or take the stopper from its mouth,
Far rather would you drink the Zakkoom juice,
And lie amid Jahennem's flames of stone,
To drag your mind from out its inward hell,   175
To outward sufferings, more to be preferred,
Than those to which remorse alone gives birth."
    King Ed-Dimiryaht took the flask, and flew
Around the works, to warn the Evil Jinn,
What woes awaited those who dared rebel,   180
Then flying swift southwestwardly, he cast
The flask away, and watched it as it sank
Deep in the salt and bitter Sea of Death,
That swallows up the Jordan, and remains
Stagnant and gloomy, edged with barren shores.   185
Four ruined cities stand upon its bed,
Where never more the voice of man shall sound.
The earthquake and volcano sleep beneath,
Their work of wrath accomplished; as the lion
Lies down, and sleeps a deep and heavy sleep,   190
When he has gorged his appetite with man.

———

CANTO II.

DAHISH.

AMID the seas between the world of men,
And that which flows within the mountain Kahf,
Are lovely islands, where the monarchs dwell,

Who rule the separate nations of the Jinn,   195
And who acknowledge as their sovereign Chief,
Iblees, or Ed-Dimiryaht.　One there was,
Who ruled a nation of the Diving Jinn, [48]
And worshipped Iblees.　In his evil days,
Zelemboor to the King an idol gave,   200
Of red carnelion, and commanded him
Daily to worship it; and as its priest,
Zelemboor bade the Efreet Dahish act.
This King ruled also o'er a race of men,
Whom he had brought to serve him, from the earth, 205
And over these he set a human King,
Whose lovely daughter worshipped constantly
The accursed idol.　When the Jinnee King
Of King Suleymahn's awful power had heard,
He sent the Efreet Dahish to his court.   210
He was a hideous Efreet, black as coal,
And of gigantic size; three fiery eyes
Glared in his face like torches; and his hair
Was as the tails of horses; and his arms
Were four in number, two like human arms,   215
Two like the legs of lions, armed with claws.
    The monster came before Suleymahn's throne,
And all the men drew backwards in affright,
And thus to King Suleymahn Dahish spoke:
"King Abd El Hahrith [49] greets you. He would fain 220
Conclude a peaceful treaty with the King
Who wears a Seal that makes the Jinn his slaves."
    "I know him not", Suleymahn made reply,
"Whom worships he, and rules he men or Jinn?"
    "He worships Iblees," Dahish fiercely cried,   225
"And to an image of his god he kneels.

Iblees has no more faithful slave than he.
He rules a mighty host of Diving Jinn,
And also rules a nation of mankind,
Whose leader serves him, and the human King,   230
Has a most lovely daughter, who adores
The idol as devoutly as myself."
    "One treaty only will I make with him,"
Suleymahn answered, "let the King proclaim,
'God is the only God in Heaven or Earth;   235
Suleymahn is his Prophet;' let him break
The idol that he worships; let him wed
To me the daughter of the human King; 50
And then will I confirm him on his throne.
But if he will not hear me, mark my words!   240
My armies of the Jinn shall fill the air,
And leave the King a thing of yesterday.
My Wezeer, Ed-Dimiryaht, shall depart,
And bring me back an answer from the King."
    Dahish bent low before the Prophet's throne,   245
And Ed-Dimiryaht with him left the hall.
Westwards they flew, and Dahish led the way
To Abd El Hahrith's island, when he asked
An audience of the King. The wicked King
With scornful indignation heard the terms.   250
"Let King Suleymahn's envoy here remain,
While I consult the god that I adore."
A Wezeer then to Abd El Hahrith spoke:
"Can King Suleymahn force you to his will?
How can he fight the armies of the Jinn,   255
Which surely will assist you? How can he
Convey his forces to your island home?
I say, resist him to the uttermost;

But first consult the idol, and abide
By what he shall direct you."
     Then the priests 260
Presented offerings to the senseless stone,
And Abd El Hahrith knelt, and weeping prayed:
"Suleymahn bids me break thee, O my lord,
And bow before another God than thee.
Assist me therefore in my need, and grant 265
Thy aid to crush the boaster to the dust."
 But Dahish crept within the hollow stone,
And spoke the oracle in lying words:
"I care not for Suleymahn! If he dares
Assail me, I will snatch his soul away. 270
Is not the future wholly in my hand?
Bring here and slay the envoy he has sent,
And send his ashes to the fool he serves,
And tell Suleymahn, 'Thy presumptuous mind
Incites thee to employ unfounded threats. 275
Come thou to me, or I will go to thee.'"
 The wicked King, when Ed-Dimiryaht came,
Repeated word for word the idol's speech.
"Suppose you," he replied, "that Iblees' troops
Can ever hope to quell Suleymahn's might? 280
Traitors, the King of the Believing Jinn
Before you stands, and he defies you all.
Behold the god in whom you put your trust!"
He spoke, and struck the idol with his foot,
And shattered it to pieces, in the midst 285
Of those indignant Chiefs, who drew their swords,
And rushed on Ed-Dimiryaht, where he stood
Alone against an army, but encased
In Jarjarees' impenetrable arms.

Uninjured to Suleymahn he returned,   290
And told his story, and Suleymahn rose,
As if his resurrection-day had come,
So great his eagerness to meet his foe.
"King Ed-Dimiryaht, call your troops of Jinn:
Assemble, Ahssaf, all my human troops;   295
For I will seek the tyrant out to-day!"
    Suleymahn spread the Carpet out, and placed
A jewelled throne of crystal first thereon,
And Ahssaf took his place upon the right,
And with him stood a million human troops.   300
As many Jinn King Ed-Dimiryaht led,
While to gain favour in Suleymahn's eyes,
Six hundred millions of the Evil Jinn
Flocked to the Prophet's standard. On the left,
Suleymahn placed the armies of the Jinn;   305
He placed the savage beasts in front of all,
And hovering o'er the army hung the birds.
At King Suleymahn's word, a mighty wind
To Abd El Hahrith's island bore his troops.
This he surrounded with his mighty host,   310
Then sent to Abd El Hahrith, "Lo, I come!
Resist me if thou darest, or submit,
And yield the terms I asked."
                    The King replied,
"I cannot yield to King Suleymahn's terms:
Inform him he must meet me in the field."   315
    Suleymahn marshalled all his troops, and spoke
First to the birds. "With talons, beak, and wings,
Assail, confuse, and blind the hostile bands,
And thus divert them from my mightier troops."
Then to the beasts he spoke. "Do ye attack   320

My foes with claws and teeth, but chiefly strive
To tear their horses down."
                         The beasts and birds
As with one voice made answer to the King:
"Prophet of God, His will and thine be done!"
On came the foe; Suleymahn gave the word,   325
And men and Jinn and beasts and birds were mixed
In one tremendous conflict. Dahish first
Against Suleymahn's army led his troops,
And Dahish said to those who round him fought:
"Maintain your places in the field. I go   330
To challenge Ed-Dimiryaht."
                           As he spoke,
The King appeared, a cloud of flaming fire,
Huge as a mountain, while the smoke arose
Wreathing in dusky columns to the sky,
Obscuring heaven, and Dahish aimed his darts   335
In vain against the King, whose spears of flame,
Struck back the darts he hurled against himself,
And Dahish found his mightiest efforts foiled.
As the pale phosphorescense of the wave,
A fire-ship quenches, so his feebler fires   340
Were quenched before his foe's o'erpowering flames.
Then Ed-Dimiryaht shouted at the fiend
A cry of war at which the mountains shook,
And Dahish thought that heaven itself had fallen,
And closed for ever o'er his sinful head.   345
    The armies met in fury, and a Chief
With Abd El Habrith closed, and pierced him through,
And rushing onward in the heat of fight,
Left him to burn to ashes. Then was heard
The clash of arms, the ceaseless roar of flames, 350

(For all the Jinn who mingled in the fight,
Were wrapped from head to foot in flames and smoke.)
With frenzied rage the hostile armies fought,
As though their very hearts within were cleft,
And in the air the birds with fury fought,   355
And in the mingled ashes, dust and blood,
Rolled horses, beasts, and men. Suleymahn cried,
"Seize ye the leaders of the Evil Jinn!"
And even while he spoke, his army charged,
And routed everywhere the hostile bands.   360
    Dahish fled westwards when he saw the rout,
And wearied with the combat as he was,
Yet thinking of Suleymahn's wrath, the fear
Urges him on with headlong speed, and swift
King Ed-Dimiryaht follows. ⁵¹ As he flies,   365
Dahish tries every means to shake him off,
But nothing can avail to save himself.
His head is dizzy, and the utmost pain
Shoots through his back and shoulders and his wings.
He falters, headlong falls, and swooping down,   370
King Ed-Dimiryaht stands above his foe.
Then Dahish spoke: "I pray thee in the name
Of Him who hath created me and thee,
And thee exalted by my shameful fall,
And since we both are Efreets of the Jinn,   375
I pray thee pity me, and let me go
To plead my cause before Suleymahn's throne."
    The pitying King responded, "Have thy will!
I cannot, Dahish harm a humbled foe,
And I will ask my master to award   380
A milder punishment than he himself
Is willing to allot you."

Dahish rose,
And went before Suleymahn. But the King,
Who would not heed the Efreet's anxious prayers,
Commands a pillar to be made of stone,   385
In which he sunk the offender to the waist,
And chained him fast, and fixed upon the chain,
His royal Seal, and Ed-Dimiryaht took
The pillar far into a waste of sand,
For Ed-Dimiryaht begged his master place   *   390
The Efreet in a pillar, not a flask.
There Abd El Melik's messengers, who went
To seek the imprisoned Efreets, saw him stand,
Chained up for evermore, aud closely watched,
Lest, spite the talisman's o'erwhelming might,   395
The crafty Efreet should attempt again
To harm Suleymahn, or Believing Jinn.

CANTO III.

THE FALL OF SIDON.

THE King of Sidon [52] with an envious eye
Beheld Suleymahn's universal sway,
And blinded by his senseless pride, he sent   400
A threatening message to him: "Would you sit
Securely on your father Dahood's throne?
Then pay to me, as guardian of your power,
An annual tribute."
                    When the envoy came,
Suleymahn heard him with a smile of scorn.   405

"Let Sidon's King beware my awful power;
Let him repeat, 'One God alone exists;
Suleymahn is his Prophet', let him give
His daughter, and the tribute asked to me."
The messenger to Sidon's King returned,   410
And gave Suleymahn's answer. He exclaimed.
"Suleymahn has defied me! He shall die,
Though all the Jinn should join him! You shall bear
This message to Suleymahn. 'Coward, come,
And raze the city Sidon to the ground!   415
Its massive walls are built of solid stone
And none can break them down!' "
                               Suleymahn heard,
And answered, "Does Suleymahn speak in vain?
The walls of Sidon may in vain oppose
Suleymahn's Carpet, or the Flying Jinn."   420
     Suleymahn spread the Carpet, and his troops
Assembled on it, when a shuddering awe
Fell upon every creature, as alone,
Through all the forces, to Suleymahn's right
A stern and silent stranger made his way; [53]   425
The troops fell back dismayed, and let him pass.
At length he stopped and gazed with moveless eyes,
Upon a Captain, who with trembling fear,
Called on Suleymahn: "Save me, thou whose power
All living things obey, for I can feel,   430
By the strange coldness creeping through my heart,
He is not human."
                     King Suleymahn rose,
And gazing on the stranger, he exclaimed,
"Who art thou stranger? Wherefore art thou here,
And wherefore dost thou stand before the man,   435

Who trembles at thy presence?"
Like a knell,

The solemn answer thrilled through every soul.
"Prophet of God, thy Seal controls not me!
Behold the angel Azraeel!"
As he spoke,

The Captain sprang and seized Suleymahn's robe.   440
"O for my childrens' sake, command the wind
To carry me to India!"
"Be it so!"

Suleymahn answered, and the obedient wind
Obeyed the implied command. Then Azraeel spoke:
"Prophet of God, thinkest thou thy mighty power   445
Can aught avail a man whose hour is come?
When Allah sent me for thy Captain's soul,
I knew that wheresoever he might be,
In India he should die!"
He spoke and fled,

And a great awe came over all the host.   450
    At length Suleymahn bade the wind uplift,
And bear his Carpet, and his valiant troops,
To Sidon, but commanded, "Men alone
Shall mingle in the fight with Sidon's troops,
For with unequal foes I will not strive."   455
    The Carpet in the heart of Sidon sank,
And Ahssaf led Suleymahn's forces on,
And lo, the King of Sidon and his troops,
Advanced against them, and the fight began.
The King of Sidon's army bravely fought,   460
But King Suleymahn's mighty force prevailed,
And slowly drove them back along the streets.
At length the King, who saw his army yield,

Cut through the foes who nearest to him fought,
And through a lane of corpses, forced his way,   465
To where Suleymahn's Wezeer, Ahssaf, fought.
Then lifting high his heavy sword, he smote
Full on the crest of Ahssaf, and the blow
Glanced from his helmet, but the Wezeer stopped, .
And rested staggering on his sword. Again   470
With all his force the King repeats the blow,
And Ahssaf drops a moment on his knees,
And from the shock recovering, shame and rage,
Alternately supply him double strength.
Then leaping to his feet, he lifts his sword,   475
And at the King he strikes. A soldier near
Opposes to the sword a weighty axe.
The ringing blade is dashed from Ahssaf's grasp,
And hurled beyond his reach. The King with joy
Beholds his foe disarmed, and once again   480
Aims a terrific blow ; beneath its force,
The tempered armour of the Wezeer yields:
His blood bedews the steel. A cry of rage
Now burst from either army; and the troops
Rushed up to aid their masters. Ahssaf sprang,   485
And seized the King, and dashed him to the ground,
When King Suleymahn's army round them thronged.
Ahssaf had now the King within his power,
And would have offered life, but while he spoke,
A Jewish spear was o'er his shoulder hurled,   490
Which pinned the hapless monarch to the earth.
"Who struck the fatal blow?" he sternly asked.
A favourite general of his own replied,
"I struck the blow, and claim my just reward."
The Wezeer seized a sword, and clove his head.   495

"So shall the Wezeer Ahssaf aye reward
The wretch who dares to strike a fallen foe!"
   The men of Sidon flung their arms away:
"We yield to King Suleymahn: grant us peace!"
Then Ahssaf bade his army cease to slay,   500
Until Suleymahn's purpose should be known.
Suleymahn answered, "Peace I grant our foes:
Their wives and children and their wealth are theirs,
For what would be the profit to myself,
To slay the troops or rob them of their wealth?   505
The city they must leave, and not rebuild:
'Twas once a stronghold of idolatry,
And I have sworn to raze it to the ground."
Ahssaf returned, and all the troops withdrew,
And King Suleymahn bade the Jinn destroy   510
The town by fire, but enter every house,
And bring before him whomsoe'er they found,
Who had not joined the army when it marched
Away from Sidon; but a furious wind
So rapidly diffused the spreading flames,   515
That hardly could the Jinn obey the King,
And snatch the few who still remained behind,
Away from burning houses, though they strove
With all their might to do the King's command.
   But in the centre of the city stood,   520
Jerahdeh, Sidon's Princess, who beheld
The flames advancing upon every side.
Upon the palace battlements she stood,
Prepared to cast herself upon the ground.
King Ed-Dimiryaht saw the flames had reached   525
The palace, and above the flames and smoke,
He flew, and seized her. Scarce his feet had touched

The battlements, when tottering to its fall,
The palace shook, and cracked, and crashed, and fell,
A fiery heap of ruins. Then the King   530
Bore to Suleymahn's tent the senseless girl,
And on returning to the burning town,
He saw the boasted walls of Sidon stand,
Blackened and scathed with fire, and all within,
A fiery sea round crashing buildings swept.   535
Suleymahn calmed Jerahdeh's wild affright,
And promised to protect her, and alone
He kept her with him; all the Sidonites
Who else were brought before him, he dismissed
To join their friends who left the town before.   540

CANTO IV.

THE REBELLION OF FAKTASH.

WHEN King Suleymahn reached Jerusalem,
He called Jerahdeh to him, and addressed
The Princess kindly: "Will you dwell with me?
I love you; will you not become my wife?
And nothing you may ask will I deny."   545
Jerahdeh answered, "True, O mighty King,
Since Sidon fell, your kindness I have proved,
Yet can I never love you."

                              "Wherefore not?
The riches of my empire all are thine."

"My father perished when the city fell.   550
O King, he was not slain at your command,
Yet how can I, a lonely orphan, love
The King who burned our dwelling to the ground,

And caused his murder?"
     From the King she turned,
And weeping hid her face with both her hands,   555
Nor would she deign to speak another word.
Suleymahn sought his private room, and called
His Wezeer Ed-Dimiryaht, and he bade
The Jinnee make a statue like the life,
Of Sidon's King, to lull Jerahdeh's grief.   560
    "Beware, O King Suleymahn," he replied,
"For fearful was the gross idolatry
That formerly in Sidon had its seat.
Be sure it can be neither right nor wise
To throw temptation in Jerahdeh's way,   565
And though I serve your Seal, I dare not risk
The danger that appears in your command.
Nor would I have you wed another wife.
Scarce passes e'en a day, unless we hear
Another Princess as your Queen proclaimed.   570
King of the world, can this be wise or right,
And must it not to countless evils lead?
Conceive you that I love Marjahneh less
Because I never wed another wife?
And yet my life ends only with the world,   575
And yours may last at most a hundred years."
    He ceased, and King Suleymahn fiercely shook
The hand which wore the Seal, above his head.
"Who dares reproach the King who owns my Seal?
Has it not power o'er every living thing?   580
If the Believing Jinn obey me not,
Send me an Efreet of the Evil Jinn:
Send Faktash, who has pleased me well of late,
And he shall be my Wezeer of the Jinn,

6*

And he shall do my bidding."
                         "Woe to thee!"   585
The Jinnee answered sternly, "Iblees waits
To take thee at thy word, O foolish King!
Art thou, the wisest of mankind, a fool?
Or knowst thou not that by thy very words,
Thou callest forth the demons of the pit,   590
And sellst thyself to work their evil will!
I can but warn thee, and perchance in vain
Mayst thou remember this!"
                         He turned his back,
And slowly and with measured steps, he strode
Out of Suleymahn's presence; and the King   595
Looked on him half remorseful; but the air
Grew dense and dark, as with a gathering storm,
And Faktash stood before him. "Trust in me,"
The Tempter cried, "I heard a rebel slave,
Oppose your royal will; but say the word,   600
And such a statue shall delight your eyes,
That if the King should rise from out his grave,
No mortal could distinguish certainly
Which figure was the King, until he moved."
     "So let it be!" Suleymahn made reply,   605
And Faktash muttered an infernal spell;
And King Suleymahn started to behold
The King of Sidon standing by his side!
And on reflection, he could scarce believe
He saw a statue, not the living King.   610
It soothed Jerahdeh's grief, and down she knelt,
And prayed before the idol when alone,
For forty days, when Abssaf sought the King,
And heard by chance the hymns Jerahdeh sung:

Then when he found the King he told him all. 615
Suleymahn rent his clothes, and beat his breast,
And imprecated curses on himself,
And called for Ed-Dimiryaht, and again
Made him his Wezeer; then he went alone
To Queen Jeradeh's chamber, and he struck. 620
The idol from its pedestal. It fell,
Shattered to pieces on the marble floor.
Then to his private chamber he withdrew,
And humbly prayed for pardon for his sin.
But Faktash took the King Suleymahn's form, 625
And passed unchallenged through the royal guards,
And sought a Queen with whom the King had left
His awful Seal, and took it. Then he clothed
Suleymahn all in rags, and made him seem
Far other from himself, his visage changed, 630
And thrust him from the palace. Faktash went
Straight to the council room, and took his seat
On King Suleymahn's throne; for e'en the Jinn
Believed the Efreet Faktash was the King.
Awhile he sat in silence; then exclaimed, 635
"The greatest of the Kings of earth am I,
And who shall dare withstand me? I adore
No God but one, and Iblees is his name,
And I command that none, on pain of death,
Shall worship any other God than he!" 640
King Ed-Dimiryaht silently arose,
And sternly on the Efreet fixed his eyes,
And Faktash quailed before his searching gaze,
And Ed-Dimiryaht knew 'twas not the King.
He took the written compact he had signed 645
With King Suleymahn, broke the seal across,

Aud tore the deed to fragments. Silent still,
He left the court with all believing Jinn.
　　By some resistless impulse that he felt
He could not master, Ahssaf tore the bond　　　　650
That both Suleymahn and himself had signed,
And cast it at the false Suleymahn's feet;
Then sprang away, and ran with all his speed
To join the Jinn before their flight commenced.
　　He could not see the army of the Jinn,　　　　655
But on the wall that fenced Jerusalem,
King Ed-Dimiryaht stood, and by his side,
Six Jinnees holding up a palankeen.
When Ahssaf joined them, Ed-Dimiryaht cried,
"A wicked Efreet has usurped the throne,　　　　660
And I must fight him at Joharahbahd.
Come with me, Ahssaf. If you stay behind,
Expect not life. He dares not follow me,
Till all the Evil Jinn increase his train.
Behold his messengers!"
　　　　　　　　　And while be spoke,　　　665
Two Efreets left the palace; one they saw
Plunge through the earth; the second bent his way
Westwards, and instantly was out of sight.
　　"Nay!" Ahssaf answered, "wherefore risk for me
Your life of centuries? No wings have I,　　　　670
And I should but impede you, and perchance
Might cause your death. O monarch, save yourself,
And think not that I fear to die. Away!
And Allah will protect me from the fiends."
　　King Ed-Dimiryaht answered not, but seized　　675
The Wezeer, cast him in the palankeen,
And from the wall he sprang; and Ahssaf looked,

And lo, Jerusalem was far away,
Lost in the distance, and the desert sands
Extended wide below him, while around   680
He saw the bearers of the palankeen
Wrapped in a halo, for so swift they flew,
He saw their wings but dimly as a mist.
The air behind them closed with thunder-roar, 54
As though 'twere parted by a lightning flash,   685
Though lightning could not equal half their speed.
    "What path, O Ed-Dimiryaht, should we take?"
The bearers asked the King, who flew above
The palankeen. He answered, "Leave behind
The grosser air of earth! The sea of blue, 55   690
Above the highest clouds will bear us best!"
    He spoke, and higher yet the Jinnees flew,
And Ahssaf looked around in trembling awe.
No sapphire vault now arched above his head:
Above, below, around him he beheld   695
A shoreless sea of deepest heavenly blue.
Panting he gazed, he could not speak or move:
His nails were purple, and with pain he breathed,
Yet as he viewed the wondrous sights around,
He did not choose to bid the Jinn descend.   700
Higher they rose, and Ahssaf senseless sunk,
And Ed-Dimiryaht bade the bearers sweep
Swift to a stratum of the denser air.
When Ahssaf looked around again, he saw
Far to the East, a pile of thunder-clouds,   705
And over these, a dazzling wall of green,
And then he knew he saw the mountain Kahf.
    King Ed-Dimiryaht placed on Ahssaf's hand
A ring, 56 and clasped him firmly in his arms.

"Away, ye Jinnees, to Joharahbahd,   710
And there await my coming!" he exclaimed.
They cast the palankeen away, and rushed
Yet swifter through the trackless sea of air,
And Ahssaf felt a sickening, rushing fall;
So swift, he lost perception as he fell,   715
Till Ed-Dimiryaht forward rushed again.
A tumult like a tempest Ahssaf heard,
Next came a single flash of blinding light,
And Ed-Dimiryaht plunged into the sea,
And placed him in the city Amberabahd.   720
  "Here stay," he cried, "the waters hurt you not
While you retain the ring. I must away
To fight the Efreet at Joharahbahd,
A city human eyes may ne'er behold."

CANTO V.

THE SIEGE OF JOHARAHBAHD.

King Ed-Dimiryaht reached Joharahbahd,   725
And both the lower diamond domes were raised,
And all assembled on the central dome
Were ranged the armies of Believing Jinn,
And even Sableh with the Diving Jinn,
Had joined King Ed-Dimiryaht's countless hosts.   730
  As Ed-Dimiryaht sank upon the dome,
A sound like thunder echoed all around,
And straight the outer dome was lifted up,
And closed above their heads. The King arose,

And he surveyed the troops, and took his stand   735
Among them near the centre. On his right
Marjahneh stood. She wore a coat of mail
Composed of diamond with asbestos fused,
Too light to hinder or impede her flight,
Yet potent to resist the fiercest flames,   740
And doubly strengthened till it turned the edge
Of scymitars, like Salah Ed-Deen's keen. [57]
   Zelemboor had his post upon the left;
His ponderous arms were formed of plated steel,
And heavier far than prudent; while the King   745
Clothed in the magic arms of Jarjarees,
Plated with massive diamonds, seemed indeed
A living tower of strength; but well he knew
No spells availed against Suleymahn's Seal!
On the left wing King Sahleh held command.   750
His arms were formed of silver, intermixed
With coral, which in rich profusion joined
To form a bright protection for the King.
   On the right wing Meymooneh had her place,
Around her stood ten thousand of her friends,   755
Virgin Jinneeyehs, who had vowed themselves
To live or die with her. The Princess stood,
Shaking her wings, and anxious for the strife,
Although she waited with a shuddering awe,
And fearful hesitation, a suspense   760
In which she longed for what she dreaded most.
She wore no armour; she had thrown aside
The coat of mail they brought her. "Bring me not
A heavy suit of armour," she exclaimed,
No arms can meet the Seal save innocence,   765
And earthly arms against a spell divine

Are blasphemous; and next to God himself,
I would place most dependence on my flames,
And on the strength and swiftness of my wings,
And not on heavy weights of steel or gems.   770
I can elude the darts that fly around,
And close with foes before they think me near,
And strike them with my sword or with my flames,
And strew their ashes on the dome below."

    She leaned upon a tempered two-edged sword,   775
Sheathless, and tightly chained around her wrist,
And she gazed up at the transparent dome,
And waited silent for the evil foes.

    The maiden's pious confidence in God,
And her bright soul, unstained by any cloud,   780
Had won the heart of Jebraeel, and he pled
Before the Throne for her, though unaware
How deeply he adored her: "Seest thou not,
O Father, how Meymooneh stands unarmed,
And unprotected save by innocence,   785
To fight the demons who possess the Seal?
Have mercy on her, Lord, and let her live,
For all who face the Seal must burn or die!"

    A milder light, yet brighter than before,
Shone forth around him. "Blessed be thy love,   790
O Jebraeel! Thine is not the sinful love,
Which Hahroot and his brother Mahroot weep.[58]
Go thou with Azraeel, and protect thy love,
For she shall be the foremost in the fight;
And gain the greatest honour in the field.   795
Yet shall she not be thine while earth remains; —
Not wholly thine, until the bridge Siraht
Unites the sons of Light, and Flame, and Earth,

In Heaven; but be her angel guardian thou!"
What glory all around Meymooneh shines!   800
She lifts her eyes, but no one near her stands,
When lo, she hears a voice remembered well,
Though unfamiliar: "Fear not, O beloved,
For I will guard thee, though thou seest me not,
And safe thou art against the Seal itself.   805
Wilt thou to Jebraeel plight eternal love?
What though we never may be one on earth,
Yet shall Israhfeel join our souls for aye.
Such love is sinless in the sight of God!"
Awhile the Princess stood oppressed with awe,   810
Trembling, afraid to speak; at length she cried,
"If, holy as thou art, thou yet canst stoop
To love a lowly daughter of the flame,
Then from henceforward I am ever thine;
Yet scarce, O Jebraeel, can I yet believe   815
That thou dost truly love me. Wilt thou wait,
Nor call me thine until in Heaven we meet?
Then, only then, will I believe thy love!"
"Peace on thee, O Meymooneh!" Jebraeel cried:
"I wait for thee until the Bridge is passed,   820
And nothing shall divide us evermore.
But now prepare to face thy deadly foes,
For lo, they all assemble on the dome!"
He ceased; but all around the Princess shone
A shining halo which the hostile darts   825
Or flames could never pierce, and now her step
Was tenfold firmer, and she shook her sword,
And called her followers, "On to victory,
For heavenly angels guard us! Fear ye not,
But do your best, and leave the rest to God!"   830

Faktash had summoned Iblees, and he came,
And all his followers with him, overjoyed
To find his servant had obtained the Seal.
Then Faktash cast away Suleymahn's shape,
And the unnumbered armies winged their way   835
Eastwards, until they lighted on the dome,
That highest rose above Joharahbahd.
The army could not find the city's gate,
And Faktash knelt upon the wall and drew
A circle with the Seal. It cut the stone,   840
As diamond, glass. The Efreet raised his haud,
And with the Seal he struck within the ring,
And all the slab within the mark was crushed.
He sprang at once with Iblees through the breach,
And all their legions followed where they led.   845
    A mighty flame flashed up between the domes,
And in the air the hostile armies met.
To meet King Ed-Dimiryaht Faktash flew,
Who hurled his spear between the Efreet's eyes,
And though no Jinnee can inflict a wound   850
On one who wears the Seal, the shock so stunned
The Efreet, that he reeled and senseless fell.
Already ashes fell as fast as rain,
And Ed-Dimiryaht knew that he must fight,
And gain such slight advantage as he could,   855
While Faktash was disabled; called his troops,
And stroke by stroke drove Iblees' army back.
When Faktash rose, he saw his army yield.
He rubbed his spear upon Suleymahn's Seal,
And hurled it at the King with all his force: 860
Nor could the arms of Jarjarees himself
Resist Suleymahn's Seal. The weapon pierced

Deep in the shoulder of the King, who fell
Helpless among the ashes, but he rose,
And snapped the spear of Faktash in the wound :   865
Then taking on the central dome his stand,
He hurled the mighty spear of Jarjarees
(Which never turned aside, or missed its aim,
And always flew again into his hand,)
Wherever he perceived the thickest foes,   870
With his left arm ; his other arm hung down
Useless ; and useless trailed his broken wing.
    Zelemboor sprang to Ed-Dimiryaht's post,
But Dahsim who observed him, hurled a spear
Which pierced him to the heart ; and as he fell   875
Marjahneh took his place. Her father came,
And furious rushed upon her ; but she quenched
Her flames, and sheathed her sword, and only sought
To turn his blows aside. He forced her back ;
And all the army wavered at the sight,   880
Uncertain whether to retreat or charge,
When darting like a rocket through the air,
Enveloped in a cloud of flaming fire,
Meymooneh rushed between them, and she struck
One blow at Dahsim with her flames. He fell,   885
And Queen Marjahneh urged her forces on,
But could not now regain the air she lost.
    Iblees advanced, and drove the army back,
And as Meymooneh for her father feared,
She called her guards, and bade them rush below   890
To seek the King, but as they wheeled, they saw
The Efreet Faktash on the central dome,
Who dashed the Seal against it, and had cleft
A fearful breach. She hesitated not,

But pointed to the hated enemy,   895
And bade her maidens sweep him from his stand,
Ere he could win the wall. They darted down,
And on their spear-points lifted up the fiend,
And hurled him far away. Meymooneh turned,
And she commanded some to hold the breach,   900
And some to bear the wounded from the fight,
And some to bid the Queen withdraw her troops,
And strive to hold the last and lowest dome.
She went to seek her father, and she took
A squadron of Jinneeyehs, and they pierced   905
Thrice through the army of the Evil Jinn.
    At length Meymooneh found herself alone,
And saw her father on the dome below
Prostrate, El Aawar kneeling on the King,
And striving through his armour-plates to force   910
A passage for his sword. El Aawar heard
A voice that cried, "El Aawar, guard thyself!"
And he by one tremendous blow was felled,
And stretched across the King. The Princess flew
So swiftly that she could not stay her flight,   915
But almost dashed herself against the dome,
For down she sank until her quivering plumes
Cast up the ashes round her. Then she dropped
Upon the dome below, and sprang again
To aid her father, when El Aawar rose,   920
And rushed against her, but she raised her sword,
And plunged it in his breast. She raised the King,
Save for the wound of Faktash' spear unhurt.
    "My father, we have lost the central dome,
And our retreat is even now cut off.   925
Our losses have been fearful, but the foe

Has also suffered greatly. Of the sons
Of Iblees, Teer and Soht alone are left;
The rest are slain. O father, lean on me,
And I will cleave a pathway for us both, 930
Amid the unnumbered foes that hem us round!"
"I cannot suffer this," the King replied.
"Go, fight as valiantly as in you lies,
But I am lost. Go, Queen of Jinneestahn,
And govern wisely those who own your power. 935
You cannot save me, and you shall not die!"
"I will not be the Queen of Jinneestahn!"
She answered firmly, "I remain with you.
Did not ten thousand maidens pledge themselves
To live or die around me? I was forced 940
To give them other duties, and in fight
Those who remained were scattered; yet I swear
By the dread Names on King Suleymahn's Seal,
I will not leave you here to die alone.
But see!" She pointed to the Evil Jinn: 945
"They charge, and we remain upon the dome,
And surely the Jinneeyehs think me lost.
O let me bear you to the lowest dome,
Else you will die, and I shall share your fate!"
    He dared no more oppose her, and she bore 950
Her father slowly and with cautious strokes,
Below the living cloud of fighting Jinn.
But suddenly the cloud was rent in twain,
And those Jinneeyehs of Meymooneh's guard
Who still survived, thronged round her, overjoyed 955
To find her living still. They fenced her well,
And guarded her, as to the lowest dome
She flew with Ed-Dimiryaht. Then she sat

Beside him, wearied with the dreadful strife,
And rested, dizzy, panting, gazing up   960
To see the fight, which seemed no longer real,
But some wild dream.
                        The Efreet forced his way
Down to the lowest dome. Marjahneh came,
And with her army fought despairingly
Against the Efreet, but she quickly fell   965
Beside the monarch, while from countless wounds
Flames flashed around her; but Meymooñeh rose,
And tore her useless sword from off her wrist,
And rushed on Faktash, and before her flames,
Or rather her protecting angel's might,   970
The Seal itself grew powerless. Faktash fled;
Then bade his army force the Princess back,
While he descended on the lowest dome.
All hope was gone if he should enter this,
Bud none could hope to stand against the Seal.   975
    But now there flashed a mighty sword of flame
Amid the evil army. Hundreds fell,
And Faktash was himself the first to fly.
Whoe'er of the Believing Jinn survived,
Was healed of all his weariness and wounds.   980
Then Azraeel thus addressed the Jinnee King:
"Attend me to Jerusalem to watch
The Efreet Faktash. None will dare again
Invade this glorious land. These shattered walls,
And hideous heaps of ashes cleanse away;   985
So shall thy kingdom grow more heavenly still!"
    When forty days had passed away, appeared
Before the throne where still the Efreet sat,
The angel Azraeel, and he shook his sword,

Threatening the fiend, and Faktash fled away.   990
He uttered one tremendous yell, and east
The Seal amid the Galilean waves.
Then Ed-Dimiryaht seized and chained him fast,
And in Suleymahn's shape assumed the throne,
Until his mighty master should return.   995
   Then the King sent for Ahssaf to returu,
And exeeute sueh duties as were his,
Ere Faktash drove Suleymahn from the throne.

CANTO VI.

THE CITY OF AMBER.

ALONE within the Amber City [59] stands
The Wezeer Ahssaf, and its golden gleam,   1000
Though dimmed by endless twilight, is as bright
As man can bear. The Diving Jinn have gone
To fight the deadliest foes of Jinneestahn;
And he, a human hero, stands alone,
At what a depth he knows not, on the bed   1005
Of that vast sea that circles round the world.
O Ahssaf, dost thou fear? An awful fate
For man to visit sueh a place as this,
It must be! Brave was Ahssaf, yet he felt
Both fear and awe. Around him he beheld   1010
Huge palaees of amber, whieh arose
High in the brightening waters, while the suns
Would gleam, perehance, upon a coral dome,
Or on a tower of amber, set with pearls.

7

Nor these were unadorned. Around them waved   1015
The sea-grass, and the gorgeous purple weeds,
And green and olive. Here the ocean zones [60]
Restrict not aught that's lovely in their bounds,
And let them rove no further; everywhere
The ocean plants are spread, and 'mid them coiled, 1020
The glorious worms of green and gold and red, [61]
Entwine their glittering rainbow-dress of hair
Among the fronds; and flowers of every hue
Expand their living petals. Surely earth
Possesses not the beauties of the sea!   1025
    And Ahssaf, as he looked on all around,
Exclaimed, "The care of God is o'er me here:
He smiles on me from all his glorious works,
And I am not alone beneath the sea!"
He knelt and prayed, not for himself alone,   1030
But for those mighty Kings, his dearest friends,
One wandering like a beggar, known to none:
One struggling with remorseless, deadly foes,
Who armed with more than demon-power, had sought
To bind the virtuous in the snares of Hell.   1035
    Then on the grass he laid him down and slept,
Exhausted by the wonders of the day,
And when he woke, he felt refreshed, and rose
Restored to strength, and walked the shining streets,
And every sight seemed lovelier than the last. 1040
    At length he reached a palace in the midst
Of Amberabahd. As far as eye could reach
Vast domes of amber and of coral rose
In the bright sparkling waters, and o'er all,
The waving splendour of the seaweeds spread;   1045
And there pourtrayed by seaweeds, shells, and flowers,

Appeared the history both of men and Jinn.
Among them, too, were mystic emblems traced,
Which stretched their meanings into future years,
And Ahssaf saw but understood them not.   1050
He saw the conflicts of a western world,
Of which he little knew; and he perceived
Emblems of future peaceful arts displayed,
Nor guessed their meanings, though with straining eyes
He sought to pierce the mysteries that they veiled, 1055
Till he was forced to look away for rest.
Bright jewels, too, abounded; but for these
The Divers cared not; and they would not change
E'en for the blinding glories than enwrap
Joharahbahd, their lovelier city here: 1060
For Amberabahd, to moonlight tempered down,
By the deep waters of the sea that flows
Within the coral reef of Jinneestahn,
Is fitter for the eyes of Diving Jinn,
Who only painfully endure the light   1065
Wherein the higher races sport and play,
With ever new and ever freshening zest.
    As Ahssaf looked on Sahleh's glorious home,
Well might he feel how weak and frail was man!
But he looked proudly up, and he exclaimed,   1070
"What if we have not now the exalted powers,
In which the angels and the Jinn rejoice?
Thank God, the life of man is but a day!
How wretched were a life of centuries
Upon the gloomy earth from whence I came!   1075
We soon should weary of a life like ours,
If it were long continued. God be praised,
The life of man is only as a day,

7*

And glories that surpass Joharahbahd,
Await us in the eternal worlds above!"   1080
   But now the fight was ended, and the Jinn
Returned to Amberabahd. King Sahleh saw
The Wezeer Ahssaf, and his guards he sent,
Commanding them to bring before his throne,
The unwonted human stranger. "Who art thou", 1085
The King demanded, "wherefore canst thou tread
The ocean waters fearlessly, and live?"
   King Sahleh spoke and Ahssaf thus replied:
"Behold Suleymahn's Wezeer, Ahssaf, here!
By Ed-Dimiryaht's influence, I defied   1090
The rebel Faktash, who possessed the Seal,
And therefore Ed-Dimiryaht placed me here,
To wait till King Suleymahn shall regain
The throne that he has lost. Behold, O King,
'Tis therefore I presume to tread unharmed   1095
The floor of ocean. — Tell me, if you know,
How went the contest at Joharahbahd?"
   "When all seemed lost, did Azracel's sword decide
The victory in our favour, yet we left
Whole squadrons of our friends in ashes laid   1100
Upon the shattered walls of adamant,
That vainly might oppose Suleymahn's Seal."
   "Does Ed-Dimiryaht live?" the Wezeer asked,
For surely he with Faktash' self would fight,
All desperate as he knew such strife to be."   1105
   "Few fought as valiantly as did the King."
He answered, "when he fought with Faktash first,
King Ed-Dimiryaht stunned him at a blow,
Although he could not wound him while he wore
Suleymahn's awful Seal; but after that,   1110

The Efreet pierced the shoulder of the King,
And Ed-Dimiryaht was not conquered then!
He stood amid the ashes, and he fought
As if he were unhurt, till Azraeel came,
And chased our foes away from Jinneestahn,   1115
And healed our wounded. One alone had strength,
Protected by a mighty angel's power,
To cope with Faktash, for she fought unarmed,
And surely we were fools to fight with arms
'Gainst that divinest spell. Meymooneh knew   1120
All arms were worse than useless, and alone
She fought against the fiend who wore the Seal,
And drove him back: all else who dared oppose
The awful spell, were wounded or were slain:
But she, who trusted only in her God,   1125
And in her pure and spotless innocence,
That never knew temptation, sin, or woe,
Prevailed against the most resistless spell,
(Though robbed of half its force in wicked hands),
That ever yet compelled our race to yield.   1130
Ahssaf, Suleymahn's Wezeer, be my guest,
For you oppose our common enemies,
And serve Suleymahn, he who rules us all;
And the Believing Jinn, aud men alike,
Are subjects of a mightier King than he!"   1135
    "I hear and I obey!" the Wezeer cried,
And I rejoice that I, although a man,
Can view your splendid city. Scarce, I deem,
Joharahbahd can boast a lovelier glow!"
    "We Divers," answered Sahleh with a smile,   1140
"Prefer our city to Joharahbahd:
But should you ask the Flying Jinn, be sure

That they will praise their glorious city most.
You can behold the glories that we love,
Around us, for our city lies entombed   1145
Deep in a tranquil sea; but never man
Shall see Joharahbahd, until the Blast
Of Consternation shakes it from its base!"
     So Ahssaf dwelt with Sahleh, and he viewed
That glorious city of the Diving Jinn: 1150
But, had he stayed in ocean all his life,
He surely could not even then have seen
One half the wonders that around him spread.
Thus quickly passed the forty days away,
When, darting through the water to the ground, 1155
King Ed-Dimiryaht's messengers arrived.
     "Ahssaf, Suleymahn is not yet restored.
But Ed-Dimiryaht occupies the throne,
Until Suleymahn shall again return.
The Efreet flung the Seal away, and waits   1160
Suleymahn's wrath in chains. We came at once,
To bid you to Jerusalem again."
     King Sahleh cried, "I also will be there,
For when Suleymahn shall regain his throne,
Perchance he needs my service. Ahssaf, go: 1165
I through the water seek Jerusalem,
Your bearers through the air, a vaster sea
Than this!"
                    The Wezeer instantly replied,
"Farewell, O Sahleh! I shall ne'er forget
The kindness you have shown me!"
                              Then he sprang 1070
Into the palankeen his bearers held,
And they at once commenced their upward course.

Now have they passed the highest amber towers,
And brighter shines the dazzling light above:
A moment, and like lightning on them burst   1175
The unclouded suns of Jinneestahn, concealed
No longer by the water; then away
The Jinnees darted to the World of Men.
Again the flash of many-coloured light:
Again the tumult of the Outer Sea: 1180
And when the Wezeer dared to raise his head,
The desert lay below him. As he gazed,
The desert vanished, and the Jinnees sank
Before Suleymahn's throne. The journey o'er,
The wondering Wezeer left the palankeen,   1185
And looked around and knew Jerusalem.

CANTO VII.

THE RESTORATION OF SULEYMAHN.

BESIDE the Sea of Galilee there sat
A fisherman, repairing broken nets.
The nets were old and worn. In vain he toiled
To mend the rents through which the fish might pass; 1190
Till, wearied by his efforts, he exclaimed,
"O Allah, pity me! I toil in vain,
For I can hardly earn my daily bread, .
And now my nets are useless, and on them
Depends my sole support : but how am I   1195
To make or purchase new ones? Must I go,
And crawling faintly to my lonely hut,
Lie down and starve for want of needful food?

) Thou, exalted o'er the Seventh Heaven,
Iave mercy on the humblest of thy sons!"   1200
  O'ercome by weariness and woe, he sank
)own on the ground, but heard a stranger's voice,
\nd saw an aged beggar standing near,
Cottering and faint with hunger.
                              "I implore
)ne morsel only of the coarsest food,   1205
\nd I will pray for blessings on your head!"
Che feeble creature cried.
                            "Alas for us!"
Che fisherman made answer, "I myself
\ttempt in vain to mend my broken nets,
\nd neither food, nor cord to mend the nets   1210
Iave I, and unassisted, I must starve,
Tis fortunate that none depend on me,
For 1 can ne'er repair my nets again:
But if you'll aid me cast them, you shall take
Che fish we capture first."
                          The beggar took   1215
Che net, and with the fisher waded in.
They cast despairingly the rotten nets,
Then drew them to the shore and spread them out,
And in the meshes lay a single fish.
The beggar seized the fish and dragged it forth,   1220
When to his joy and wonder, from its mouth
A glittering ring fell down.
                            "O God be praised!"
The beggar cried, for King Suleymahn spoke,
"Behold my long-lost Seal at length restored!
O fisherman, farewell to toil and care,   1225
For King Suleymahn wears his Seal again,

And well will he your charity reward!"
The fisherman replied not when he heard
The King proclaim himself, for well he thought
The ring they found had made him mad with joy: 1230
But King Suleymahn lifted up the Seal,
And placed it on his finger, and his form
And kingly bearing was at once restored.
Then south towards Jerusalem he looked,
And he looked eastwards towards Jinneestahn,   1235
Then with commanding gesture stretched his hand,
And pointing with the finger that sustained
The talisman, exclaimed, "A human King
Commands thy presence, King of Jinneestahn!
Where'er thou art, obey the spell divine,   1240
O Ed-Dimiryaht, for Suleymahn's self
Invokes thee!"
                Scarcely had he called his name,
When Ed-Dimiryaht by his master stood.
Amazed the fisherman beheld the Kings,
And rooted to the ground in joy and fear,   1245
Stood gazing silently. At length he heard
Suleymahn speak again: "Now tell me, King,
How matters went with you, and with my realm."
King Ed-Dimiryaht answered, "In his chains,
Writhing and cursing and blaspheming lies   1250
The Efreet Faktash. Azraeel rescued us,
Who else had yielded to the powers of Hell,
And Azraeel drove the Efreet from your throne:
I filled it since, awaiting your return."
    "Convey me quickly homewards; then shall I   1255
Give Faktash cause to rue his transient reign:
And bring the fisherman to whom I owe

The power I lost."
                    Then Ed-Dimiryaht called
A Jinnee, and commanded him to bear
The fisherman to King Suleymahn's court;   1260
While he himself caught King Suleymahn up,
And in Jerusalem he set him down.
    Suleymahn on the fisherman bestowed
Abundant honours and enormous wealth:
Then he to Ed-Dimiryaht turned, and cried: 1265
"Bring here the Efreet Faktash in his chains!"
The King withdrew, then wide he flung the door,
And cast the struggling Efreet on the ground
Before Suleymahn, and the palace shook
With the loud clangour of the mighty chains,   1270
And with the howls and curses of the fiend.
Suleymahn viewed him with an angry frown,
And a stern anger gleaming in his eye,
That showed the Efreet that escape was none.
    "Bring here," Suleymahn cried, "a monstrous stone, 1275
And chain it firmly to the Efreet's neck!"
And as he spoke, the King performed the work,
And every limb of Faktash wore a chain,
And every chain was linked to all the rest,
And Faktash lay enclosed in iron bands,   1280
Which formed a network round him, while he strove
In vain to move a limb; and, on his neck,
A monstrous block of stone was hung, secured
By chains as massive as the rest. He lay
Writhing, and struggling helplessly to break   1285
The ponderous chains, for all his power was gone.
Then King Suleymahn on the Efreet knelt,
And on the stone and chains impressed his Seal.

He rose and looked at Faktash: "There you lie!
And never, traitor, shall the chains be loosed,   1290
For in the sea that over Sodom flows, [62]
Shall Ed-Dimiryaht cast you, O accursed!
The horrors of that awful Sea of Death,
Are all that you shall ever see or hear;
And neither leg, nor arm, nor wing can move   1295
Beneath the weight of these enormous chains;
And, till Israhfeel's Second Trumpet sounds,
There shall you lie, and all who hear your fate,
Shall tremble and beware Suleymahn's might,
Nor ever dare to fight against the Seal!"   1300
   As thus he spoke, King Ed-Dimiryaht seized
The Efreet's chains, and raised him from the ground,
And bore him southwards, and at length he reached
The Sea of Death, and let the Efreet fall.
   Down in the sea the helpless Efreet fell,   1305
And sank beneath the torpid waves that closed
Above him. Down he sank, until he lay
On a high temple that was half consumed,
And where himself in ages long forgot,
Had bid the nations worship him. He knew   1310
The temple, and he seemed to see again
The crowds that knelt before him; and again
He heard their hymns. The dead had sprung to life,
And on the bed of that accursed sea,
E'en then were suffering torments for their sins.   1315
   They knew the Efreet, and saluted him:
"O welcome, Faktash, to the Sea of Death!
Praise to the mighty hero, foiled at last,
By Azraeel's puny might! Can Azraeel harm?
Lo, Faktash, here we reign for evermore: 1320

Our only joy is felt in others woe,
And those who make us feel the greatest pain,
We worship. Die, O Faktash, in the name
Of Iblees the Accursed; yet return
To life once more, to suffer ceaseless pains,   1325
Until the Second Trumpet shall be heard!"
　One mighty effort Faktash made, and tore
His body piecemeal from the iron net,
And, as his sinful soul was hurled away,
His body burned to ashes, though beneath   1330
The stagnant waters of that earthly Hell,
And Faktash stood among his ancient dupes,
And saw his body burning, till it lay
Consumed to ashes, which the sea dispersed,
And wheresoe'er the accursed ashes touched,   1335
They burned as bluely heated. But behold!
Above their heads, the ancient Sodom rose,
And all who saw it yelled with fear and rage:
There stood the stately home of every sin;
When lo, a fearful cry of woe was heard,   1340
And the volcanic caverns at their feet
Burst open, and the burning lava rose,
Shot up above the city's loftiest towers,
And overwhelmed the crowds who stood below.
Then with a fearful crash the city fell,   1345
And in its heated ruins it entombed
Again its old inhabitants. Once more
The city rose; again the lava springs
Wrapped it in liquid flame. Thus Sodom burns
Eternally with flames that nought may quench,   1350
Until the Second Trumpet's sound is heard.

CANTO VIII.

THE QUEEN OF SEBA.

SULEYMAHN marched to Mekkeh with his troops, [63]
And turned again towards Jerusalem,
And halting in the desert, he surveyed
The army of the birds. They passed him by,   1355
And he exclaimed, "The Lapwing, where is she?
My armies need refreshment; where is she
Who shows us where the hidden waters lie?
Unless she fairly answers for delay,
She dies!"
        But e'en as King Suleymahn spake,   1360
The Lapwing came before him, and she bent
Her head in deprecation of his wrath,
And he forgave her.
        "Lapwing", said the King,
"I waited long expecting your return,
For water was there none that we could find,   1365
And all my wearied army long to drink.
Acquaint me with the cause of your delay."
    The Lapwing answered, "In El Yemen dwells
A Queen more beautiful and wise than all
That dwell with thee in proud Jerusalem,   1370
And I delayed to learn her name and state.
Her throne is gold and silver, half concealed
By gems like those that gleam eternally,
Beneath the brilliant suns of Jinneestahn.
Yet Bilkees [64] Queen of Seba, knows not God,   1375
For she adores the sun, and never heard
How brilliantly the Throne of Allah shines,

Which even the Archangels scarce can bear!"
  Suleymahn answered, "I resolve to march
My army thither, but delay awhile,   1380
And show us where the hidden waters lie:
Then guide us to the Queen of whom you speak!"
  The Lapwing led the Prophet to a well,
And all the army drank and quenched their thirst,
And as Suleymahn rested by the well,   1385
He called for pen and paper, and he wrote:
"To Bilkees, Queen of Seba, in the name
Of Heaven's eternal Ruler, from a king,
And Prophet of the Mightiest; even he,
Suleymahn, son of Dahood, who alone   1390
Of living men, shall wear a Seal divine,
On which the name of God himself is stamped. —
All rulers are the servants of the Lord,
And all should learn to rule their people well,
And form alliances with friendly Kings,   1395
Nor should reject their friendship. I invite
Your presence, Bilkees, at Jerusalem,
Attended by an escort, all composed
Of men, the wisest that your realm contains;
For on its wisdom, not its wealth, depends   1400
The welfare of a nation."
                              Then he gave
The letter to the Lapwing. "Cast it down
Before the Queen, and swift return to me,
For now we seek again Jerusalem!"
  When King Suleymahn reached Jerusalem,   1405
He ordered Ed-Dimiryaht to construct
A spacious palace floored with limpid glass, [65]
While water flowed beneath it, where were placed

Fishes of every species.
                          Bilkees sat
Among her courtiers, when a letter sealed   1410
Fell in her lap. She trembled as she read,
And asked her nobles for advice; but none
Presumed to give an answer; then she spoke:
"Kings waste a country weaker than their own,
And surely King Suleymahn means me ill;   1415
But I will send a present to the King,
And if a Prophet, he will send it back,
And if he's but a King, I buy him off!"
     Suleymahn viewed her presents with disdain,
And answered those who brought them, "Take them
                                         back: 1420
Look round and view my treasures! Did I ask
A present from her? I demand from her
Her friendship, not her treasures, yet she dares
Insult me by a present! Bid her come
In fullest confidence, and fear no ill!"   1425
     Queen Bilkees in her palace left her throne,
Secured by fifty doors of solid steel,
And every door secured by fifty locks,
And all indignant at Suleymahn's slight,
She led her troops against Jerusalem.   1430
Around her marched twelve thousand subject Kings,
And each brought thousands of his choicest troops.
     Suleymahn asked his courtiers, "Who will fetch
The throne of Bilkees?"   .
                          "I", an Efreet [66] cried,
"Ere from your throne you rise."
                          The King replied, 1435
"I wish to see the throne before me now;"

And Abssaf answered, "I will bring it here,
Ere, having fixed your eyes upon the sky,
You look again towards me."
                              "Be it so!"
Suleymàhn answered, and the Wezeer rose,   1440
And he invoked the Name upon the Seal,
And lo, the throne before Suleymahn stood.
    Then, turning to the Efreet, said the King:
"Place this in Bilkees' palace floored with glass,
And overlay it all with priceless gems,   1445
To hide the gold and silver, not concealed
By those which Bilkees lavished on her throne.
Will she believe her throne is brought to us,
And altered, or deny that this is hers?"
    A Jinnee entered as Suleymahn spoke,   1450
And told the King that Bilkees led her hosts
Prepared to fight against him. "Vain her wrath",
Suleymahn answered calmly, speaking now
To Ed-Dimiryaht. "Dig a mighty gulf
A thousand fathoms deep, and lined with gold,   1455
Around the city. Let Meymooneh go,
To bear the Queen alone across the gulf:
For Bilkees shall not lead her army here,
Except by my permission, till she learns
The might of those who worship God aright,   1460
And whom he deigns to honour. Let her leave
Her Kings and her attendants, and alone
Here seek me."
                    Ed Dimiryaht bade his troops
Commence the work Suleymahn had designed,
And he himself flew eastward, to instruct   1465
His daughter to fulfil the King's commands.

The Queen rode on before her mighty host,
And saw a gleaming thread of gold that stretched
Amid the hills on which the city stood;
But no one could inform her what it meant,   1470
Until they reached the gulf. A cry of fear
Burst from the troops, for well they knew they saw
No human work before them.

                  "Pitch me here,"
The Queen exclaimed, "a tent beside the gulf,
And ride around the gulf, until you find   1475
An entrance to the city."

                  There she sat,
Until a King, who galloped round the gulf,
Returned and cried, "Alas, we cannot fight:
Securely King Suleymahn's barred access
To his proud city!"

                "He despises us!"   1480
Cried Bilkees fiercely, "yet he dares not fight,
But I will wipe his insults out in blood!"

   As Bilkees spoke, she saw Meymooneh flash
Before her, as she stood by Thora once,
Yet lovelier now than then, for now there shone   1485.
A shimmering lustre of the light of Heaven
Around her, sign of Jebraeel's care and love,
Where'er Meymooneh strayed.

               "O fear not, Queen!"
The Princess cried, "for King Suleymahn ne'er
Despised you as you think. He only asks   1490
That you should come submissively to him,
And therefore will he not admit your troops,
But bids me bear you o'er the gulf alone.
Bid all your host encamp, and come with me,

And I will bear you to Jerusalem."   1495
   At this the King advanced, and drew his sword:
"I fear you not, Jinneeyeh, and the Queen
Shall never go with you!"
                     She caught the blade,
And round her hand she twisted it, unhurt,
The metal dripping melted from her grasp,   1500
And wrenched it from him with a force that sent
The monarch reeling twenty paces back:
Then, as she flung the shreds into the gulf,
"Begone!" she cried, "and leave us here alone:
My errand is to Bilkees, not to you!"   1505
The King departed conquered and ashamed,
While Bilkees pondered o'er Meymoonch's words.
At length she cried, "Jinneeyeh, will you swear,
By that great Name to King Suleymahn known,
That neither he nor you will do me hurt?   1510
Then will I go with you."
                  Meymooneh took
The oath she could not break, and spoke again:
"Nay, never fear, for I will bear you safe
E'en to the palace King Suleymahn's self
Has built for you; but leave your troops behind.   1515
The daughter of the King of Jinneestahn
Am I, and wherefore should you feel afraid,
Since I have sworn your safety on the Seal?"
   As she was speaking to the Queen, she loosed
Her tresses, wreathed with many an odorous flower;   1520
And when from this delicious bondage freed,
O'er her bright plumage to her feet they flowed.
"Grasp my long hair [67], and fear not!" As she spoke,
Queen Bilkees grasped her hair, and by its aid

Climbed on her shoulders, and Meymooneh stepped 1525
Close to the deep abyss, and fearlessly
Gazed in the awful gulf; and Bilkes' heart
Failed her. "Jinneeyeh, I am sick and faint!
I cannot bear to cross this dreadful pit,
And if I fell, I could not hope for life!"   1530
   Meymooneh grasped the Queen with both her hands:
"I know not what you feel when you behold
A deep abyss like this; but as for me,
It moves me not. I will not let you fall.
I wish you first to view Jerusalem,   1535
Before you touch the city, from the air.
But shrink not from the height, for I am safe,
And by the Seal I swear you shall not fall!"
   She spoke, and sprang with Bilkees o'er the gulf,
And Bilkees held her with convulsive fear,   1540
Smooth as she flew; but when the Princess rose
Above the splendid city, all her dread,
Was changed to wonder. She was overjoyed
When as she gazed, Meymooneh bade her view
The stately palace built for her alone.   1545
Meymooneh cared not to descend at once:
She circled round Jerusalem, and sank
With Bilkees slowly at the palace gate.
Meymooneh waited till Suleymahn came:
Then bent before the King, and disappeared.   1550
Suleymahn bade the Queen ascend the steps
And view the spacious palace. When she reached
The entrance-hall, she raised her dress to wade
Through water, but she set her feet on glass.
   "Behold the power that God bestows on those", 1555
The King exclaimed, "who worship him aright!

O Bilkees, do you deem this throne your own?"
She answered, " 'Tis the same, and not the same."
    "Queen," King Suleymahn cried, "God bade me lead
To him the race of men. Submit to him,   1560
And he will honour thee if thou will say,
God is the only God in Heaven or earth:
Suleymahn is his Prophet!"
                     Bilkees spoke
The words that he commanded, and awhile
He stood in silence; then he spoke again: 1565
"Believe not, Queen, I ever wished you ill:
I but designed to show how great the might
Of those who worship Allah, and how weak
Were infidels against them. I perceive
A wisdom equal to my own in thee,   1570
And offer now to wed thee, so shall we
So fitted to each other, wisely act;
Thyself the wisest of all earthly Queens,
And I the single Ruler of the earth,
For all believing rulers bow to me,   1575
And not an unbelieving King survives,
Who qnakes not at my name; and tell me not
That you may feel unworthy of my love,
If I esteem you worthy, deem yourself
A fitting consort for me. Speak the word,   1580
And I will bid my officers attend,
And let your army enter as they list,
And we will be united in this hall.
But if you will not wed me, then return
Unharmed with all your army, and demand   1585
Suleymahn's aid when he can give you aught."
    The Queen objected not; the gulf was filled,

And all her army marched into the town,
And they were much rejoiced when first they heard
That King Suleymahn wished to wed their Queen. 1590
  Suleymahn wedded Bilkees, and returned
With her to where she dwelt, and stayed a month,
And all the nation feasted day and night,
Till his departure to Jerusalem.
Thenceforth Suleymahn passed a week with her   1595
In every month, and prosperously she ruled
For years, possessing all she could desire,
For all she needed, King Suleymahn gave.

———

CANTO IX.

THE VISIONS OF AHSSAF.

AHSSAF looked back with awe upon the time,
When, on the palaces of Amberabahd,   1600
He saw the future destinies of the earth.
Whene'er he was alone, before his eyes
The vague and mystic prophecies appeared,
Although he strove in vain to read the signs,
And Sahleh would not give the slightest hint,   1605
Concerning what the mystic symbols meant.
  One evening he had pondered anxiously,
On what should prove his country's final doom;
Till, wearied by his fruitless waste of thought,
He sank upon a couch, and fell asleep.   1610
Jerusalem appeared before his eyes,
O'ershadowed by a mighty Eagle's wings,
Crumbling to dust! He started to his feet,

And in the wild dismay that filled his soul,
He uttered first the mystic Name of God,   1615
Then called the King of the Believing Jinn.

    King Ed-Dimiryaht heard the spell divine,
And stood before the Wezeer. "O my friend,
Why call my name in such a tone of fear?"
He asked, "have Iblees' troops again contrived   1620
To steal Suleymahn's Seal? Or has the King
Himself alarmed you with unwelcome news,
Or acted foolishly, and cast himself
Again upon the mercy of his foes?"

    "Not so!" said Ahssaf, trembling as he told   1625
His fearful dream. "O King, if power is yours,
Reveal to me the future destinies
That wait the mightiest nations of the earth."

    "I have the power," the King replied; "but come,
And you shall view a mystic glass that lies   1630
Beneath the Temple's lowest court concealed."

    Ahssaf sprang up, and walked beside the King
Along the lonely streets. At length they reached
The Temple, where the Jinn were working still,
And Ed-Dimiryaht led the Wezeer on,   1635
Through one grand court, and down a flight of steps,
That brought them to the Temple's basement floor.

    King Ed-Dimiryaht looked upon the ground,
And carefully surveyed the massive stones,
Then as he found the one he sought, he stooped,   1640
And wrenched it from the pavement with a force
That shook the mighty Temple to the roof.
He flung the stone above him, and he seized
The Wezeer, and he sprang into the well
The stone had closed, and when it fell, its weight, 1645

Secured it in its place. He darted down,
As though he wished to reach the Seventh Earth;
But suddenly he checked himself, and set
The Wezeer Ahssaf on his feet again.
He led him through a cavern dark and damp,   1650
Until they reached a room with granite walls,
Where a great mirror hung. The King exclaimed,
"Now, Ahssaf, put your questions to the glass,
And it shall answer, far as 'tis allowed
To human eyes to view futurity."   1655
     "Tell me," said Ahssaf, "shall Jerusalem
Remain the greatest city of the earth,
And shall a long and prosperous race of Kings
Succeed Suleymahn?"
                    In the glass he saw
The very Eagle of his dream appear   1660
Distinct before him, and he spoke again:
"May I behold the sins by which we fall?"
     Then all the mirror reddened, and it streamed
With blood, as though the senseless glass itself,
Wept for the sin and woe of Palestine!   1665
     "Lo", Ed-Dimiryaht cried, "you may not see
Your country's ruin plainer, but demand
To see the mighty nations which shall rise,
When Palestine shall fall before the might
Of that dread nation yet unborn, that rose   1670
An Eagle to your vision."
                         Ahssaf cried,
"Let me behold the Eagle and its doom,
For when the measure of its crimes is full,
Shall not the Eagle fall?"
                         He looked, and saw

The Eagle resting on a lofty hill,   1675
Where seven high peaks arose. The Eagle spread
Wide its black wings, and wider still they grew,
And whensoc'er the Eagle waved its wings,
A rain of blood fell round it. They beheld,
Till the fierce Eagle buried in its breast,   1680
Its own blood-reeking bill, and faintly strove
To keep its claws firm planted on the hill.
    But now a Raven came, and fiercely rushed
Against the exhausted Eagle, from the North,
And tore the longest feathers from its wings ;   1685
Then trod it down upon its rocky throne,
And utterly o'erthrew it, though it cast
A gloomy darkness round it as it fell,
That wrapped its limbs around, and cast a shade
That fell upon the Raven, and the plumes   1690
The Raven tore away. A Lion sprang
From out the Raven's beak, and quickly grew
Far larger than the Eagle (which was dead,
And cast a gloom o'er all); and silently,
The crown that fell from off the Eagle's head,   1695
When it had pierced its breast, upraised itself,
And stood abowe the Lion, o'er whose head
The conquering Raven spread its wings of night.
The Raven saw the darkness which arose
From the dead Eagle, and oppressed itself   1700
Whit an unnatural weight. The Raven rose,
And with the Lion's aid, it quite dispelled
The thickest gloom for ever.
                              "You have seen
The greatest nations that shall next arise,
When falls Jerusalem," the King exclaimed: 1705

"Would you see more?"
"Alas," said Ahssaf," nay.
I would not see more ruin. I perceive
No human nation e'er can long endure,
And I should only see the Lion fall,
And perhaps a mightier power than his, arise   1710
And fall again. I would not longer view,
The alternating nations of the earth.
I sure was wrong to ask it. for I feel
The hinted ruin of Jerusalem,
Will weigh upon my happiness till death!"   1715
  "'Tis wise!" said Ed-Dimiryaht, "not a race
Shall ever rise that shall not also fall;
And did we not beyond the present gaze,
And see a distant future, brighter far,
Most gloomy were the thought!"
         A darkening cloud 1720
O'ershadowed now the mirror, and the King
Led Ahssaf through the caverns, till he seized
The Wezeer in his•arms, and bore him up;
Then lifting once again the massive stone,
He led him through the Temple. Ahssaf walked   1725
In silence to his home, for he perceived
Too surely that Jerusalem must fall.

<hr>

CANTO X.

THE DEATH OF SULEYMAHN.

. In love and war Suleymahn passed his days,
But e'en the wisest of mankind must die:
And sixty [68] years had fled since first the King   1730

Had mounted Dahood's throne. Before the Seal,
All living things bowed down. Suleymahn ruled
Alone and unopposed, from Kahf to Kahf.
  One evening King Suleymahn sat alone,
Attended only by his faithful friends,   1735
His wezeers, in the hall where first the three
Had sworn eternal friendship on the Seal.
Three youths they were who swore, but see them now!
Suleymahn's hair was grey, his strength was gone,
His senses failing, and his mind impaired.   1740
Ahssaf, the aged man upon the right,
Was older than the King; his hair was white;
His form was bowed with age; his eyes were dim,
And he could hardly walk across the hall.
Alone unaltered, in eternal youth,   1745
As changeless as unchanged, upon the left,
Stood Ed-Dimiryaht, gazing mournfully
Upon the friends he knew he soon must lose.
  At length Suleymahn spoke: "Lo, I am old,
And after me Jerusalem shall fall;   1750
No King so great shall ever rule again,
For man shall never more possess my Seal.
Alas, the Temple is not yet complete,
And much I fear I shall not see it stand
Exalted in the glory that I hoped,   1755
And then the crowning glory of my reign,
I never shall attain to."
                       "Trust in God,"
Replied the Wezeer Ahssaf, "trust in God;
For he has power to hide your death from those
Who work beneath the terror of the Seal.   1760
Lo, King Suleymahn, I am older still,

And weaker than yourself; but why should we
Quail at the thought of death? Have we not kuown
Such revelations of the will of God,
As few beside have known? I do not fear   1765
A fate no human power can e'er evade;
And when I pray to God in greatest joy,
I thank him for the shortness of our lives!"
   Then Ed-Dimiryaht spoke. "I long have sought
To know the mysteries of your race of earth.   1770
My life of centuries, as I perceive,
Is less to me than is a year to you;
But when the Second Trumpet's sound is heard,
I shall not shrink from death, for well I know,
A higher life awaits me; and do you,   1775
Creatures of earth, who live a century,
Or oftener less; you whom no power can save
From sin and suffering; you who cannot move
Far from the spot where you were born; who know
From your experience nought of other worlds;   1780
Do you regret to die, and leave behind
The greatest earthly splendours, which are nought?
Shall not Joharahbahd itself sink down,
When the First Trumpet sounds? Yet which of you
Could bear to gaze a moment on the light   1785
That wraps the Jewel City like the air?
I never yet could comprehend your race,
But strangest to me is your fear of death!"
   Suleymahn lifted up his mighty Seal,
And spoke to Ed-Dimiryaht. "You, O King,   1790
Have served me faithfully, and you indeed
Have kept the oath you swore upon the Seal,
When I and Ahssaf both were young as you.

Unaltered still you seem, but as for us,
You see how aged and how weak we are.   1795
Our faith is weakened by our failing health,
But still our souls are faithful in themselves."
      He spoke, and all the lamps around were dimmed,
By a resplendent light that filled the hall;
And lo, before the Prophet, clothed in light,   1800
The Archangel Jebraeel stood, his glory veiled
Sufficiently for human eyes to bear!
"Prophet of God, Suleymahn!" he exclaimed,
To-morrow you shall sink into a sleep
From which Israhfeel's Trumpet bids you rise.   1805
Lean on your staff, and on the Temple gaze, [69]
And you shall stand as living, for a year,
Till it shall stand in all its lofty pride,
As you would wish to see the crowning fame,
That overhangs your life eternally,   1810
Though future ages may dispute your deeds.
Ahssaf shall live to see the finished work,
And then shall die. O monarch of the Jinn!
Upon his throne the Prophet thou shalt place,
And seek a cavern in a lonely isle,   1815
Far distant from the homes of men and Jinn,
Amid the Outer Sea. There shalt thou place
Suleymahn, and beside him Ahssaf too,
And God shall send a Serpent, which shall guard
The Seal, until the Spy [70] shall come to mark   1820
The true believers all with Moosa's Rod,
And unbelievers with Suleymahn's Seal."
      Suleymahn heard and answered, "It is well!
What worth were life without eternal youth,
Like thine, or Ed-Dimiryaht's? I am old,   1825

And every pleasure palls upon my sense.
Ahssaf is happier than myself: he looks,
In trusting faith, which I can ne'er attain,
With joy beyond the fearful Bridge of Breadth."
"Peace be to thee, and to thy wezeers both,"   1830
The angel answered, "Ahssaf, do not mourn,
Though thou shalt live another year at least.
Before the Bridge you meet the King again,
Nor shall you e'er be parted after that!"
He spoke, and speaking vanished from their sight, 1835
And King Suleymahn said, "Remain with me:
For since, O wezeers, we so soon must part,
I will not sleep again!"
                              The wezeers stayed
Until the morning dawned. Suleymahn rose,
And by his wezeers still attended, walked   1840.
Around the city; then he climbed a hill
Front whence he saw the Temple towering rise,
Near to him in its splendour. On his staff
He leaned, and spoke to Ahssaf, but he spoke
So low, so very low, and fainter still,   1845
That Ahssaf rather felt than heard the words:
"A dizziness comes o'er me: I perceive
The Temple slowly fading from my sight:
I do not feel as standing; and my hands
That rest upon the staff, perceive it not.   1850
I feel as though suspended in the air,
Thick darkness closing round me, while the sound
Of those employed upon the Temple, fails
To reach my ears. The only feeling left,
Is consciousness, and even consciousness,   1855
Is fading from me."

            Still he moved his lips,
But not a word they heard. The Prophet stood
Between his wezeers, lifeless. They perceived
The King was dead, but they concealed his death,
Till the last stone was lifted to its place.   1860
Then fell the King, and the rebellious Jinn,
Perceived that he was dead, and they had toiled
In fear of one who could not harm them more.
Ahssaf survived not long, and when he died,
The King of the Believing Jinn conveyed   1865
The lifeless bodies to a lonely isle.
There Ahssaf and Suleymahn ever sit,
Protected by a Serpent sent by God, [71]
To guard the awful Seal from hands profane.
    Then Ed-Dimiryaht sought Joharahbahd,   1870
To cleanse the city from all trace of war.

END OF THE THIRD BOOK.

BOOK THE FOURTH.
THE FOUNTAIN OF YOUTH.

ARGUMENT.

I. The Affairs of Jinneestahn. Iskender's expedition in search of the Fountain of Youth. He calls a council. Israhfeel forbids Ed-Dimiryaht to interfere. Iskender's adventures in the cave. His interview with Israhfeel. Death of Iskender.

II. El Khidr and Ilyahs meet in the cave. Discovery of the Fountain. Appearance of Israhfeel. Return of the Brothers to the camp of Iskender. The cavern closes.

CANTO I.

THE EXPEDITION OF ISKENDER.

KING Ed-Dimiryaht quickly cleared away
The shattered walls of diamond, useless now,
And all the heaps of ashes, scattered still
Among the broken walls. The Evil Jinn
Would never venture near the city more,   5
And nothing now could dim its dazzling light.
The brightest earthly noon could never vie

With midnight splendour at Joharahbahd;
And even Amberabahd had now attained
A glory far too bright for eyes of man.   10
Still Ed-Dimiryaht and his subjects strove
To interfere for good in human acts,
And Iblees and his evil army dared
No longer to molest them in their work.
At evening the Believing Jinn who sought   15
The world of men, returned to tell their deeds,
With pride that none could blame; and each received
His praise deserved; and thus in acts of love,
Of others thinking, rather 'than themselves,
Their earthly joys resemble those of Heaven.   20
    But centuries had come and passed away
Since King Suleymahn's death. Iskender's [72] deeds
Had now become renowned. A Jinnee came
From King Iskender's camp, to which he went
To strive to guide the King to milder acts;   25
And he to Ed-Dimiryaht told his tale,
How that the King Iskender had resolved,
Within the caverns of the Caucasus,
To seek the Fountain of Eternal Youth.
    "Then I myself must seek his camp," he cried: 30
"Although I greatly doubt if Allah wills
That Jinn should interfere in this at all.
You acted rightly to repair to me,
Unknowing how you should direct the King!
Await me on the Coral Reef awhile,   35
For I would speak to you again of this,
When I return."
                    He spoke, and he was gone.
Iskender with his Chiefs in council sat,

As Ed-Dimiryaht went invisibly
Among the Chiefs. At length Iskender spoke: 40
"You know, my heroes, why I bade you.meet.
Can no one here unfold the mysteries hid
In that tremendous cave? Has ever man
Explored the cave, or tasted of the spring?"
     "Dark is the cave, with many a winding maze,"   45
A Captain answered; "none could ever pierce
The deeper windings of that cavern vast,
For if they ventured far, they ne'er returned.
Unless you could observe the path you took,
You sure would wander in that frightful cave,   50
Nor ever see the cheerful light again,
But die at length from hunger, or perchance
The deep abysses that the cave conceals
Would swallow you, for horrors infinite
Await the unwary wanderer in its gloom."   55
     Iskender once again addressed his Chiefs:
"Is there an aged man in all the camp,
On whose advice I safely might depend?
I dare not trust to youths in such a case,
Yet have I left my veterans far away,   60
In strongly guarded forts."
                              A soldier rose,
Ilyahs [73] by name. "My brother and myself
Have brought our father with us, for we feared
Lest dangers should beset him, while we marched
Far distant from the city where he dwelt."   65
     "Then call your father and your brother here,"
Iskender answered. Ilyahs sought his tent,
And soon he brought them both before the King;
And Ilyahs' father to Iskender spoke:

9

"O King, the cave will surely be your tomb,   70
Unless you ride a mare, and bind her colt
Hard by the cavern's mouth; and she will trace
Her backward pathway safely to the light."
    So spoke the Sheykh; and though he knew it not,
The King of Jinneestahn the thought inspired.   75
    "Enough!" Iskender answered, "I will take
El Khidr and Ilyahs with me in the cave,
Alone of all my army."
                    Then he rose,
And to the dismal cave he led his troops,
Attended by King Ed-Dimiryaht still.   80
    But by no eyes but Ed-Dimiryaht's seen,
Israhfeel, who shall sound the Trump of Doom,
Descended.
            "King, 'tis given to me alone,
To guard the sacred Fount, so Allah wills."
    King Ed-Dimiryaht bowed submissively   85
Before the Archangel, and he left the cave.
Iskender, when he reached the cavern's mouth,
Made all his troops encamp. Alone he took
El Khidr and Ilyahs with him, and they rode
Each on a mare whose colt was bound without.   90
They soon arrived where branched the path in three:
Iskender chose the centre; Ilyahs took
The right path, and El Khadir took the left.
Iskender shunned the smaller roads, and took
The path that always broadest seemed to him.   95
At length he reached a door of polished steel,
To which a bird was fastened.
                        "Whó art thou,"
It asked Iskender, "and what dost thou here?"

"Lo, King Iskender answers! Here I seek
The Fountain of Eternal Youth."
                                .   The bird   100
Responded, "Doth the world fare well or ill?"
The King replied, "The world o'erflows with woe:
'Tis caused by sins whose aggregate is such,
No mortal could declare the fearful list!"
    He spoke; the bird was loosed, and as it fled,   105
With one tremendous clang, the gate of steel
Rolled back, and opened wide. The King beheld
Israhfeel, with the Trumpet in his hand.
    "Who art thou?" cried the King.
                                "Israhfeel stands
Before thee. See the Trumpet that I bear!   110
Thrice must its thunder burst o'er every world,
But thou shalt hear it once, and once alone!
I know thee, King, and what thou seekest here!"
Thereat he took a pebble from the ground.
    "When thou shalt find a stone of equal weight,   115
Presumptuous man, eternal youth is thine!"
    "Israhfeel, tell me when my life shall end?"
    "Thy life shall last until thy heavens and earth
Be turned to iron."
                            Iskender took the stone,
And left the cave, supposing all was gained.   120
Long time he sought, but never could obtain
A stone of equal weight. At length a stone
Scarce varied in the balance. Then he took
Some earth, and made it even; but he failed
To read the meaning that his act involved: 125
"Till thou thyself art yielded to the earth,
O mortal, hope not for eternal youth!"

Soon after this, Iskender chaneed to ride
Across a desert, and his charger fell,
And he was sorely bruised. His soldiers laid   130
Iskender in his armour on the ground,
And o'er him hung his buckler, to protect
The monarch from the burning Eastern sun.
Iskender soon perceived his heavens and earth
Were built of iron; and now remembered well   135
The earth that in the balances he placed,
And knew that he must die; his eyelids closed;
His head sank back; he strove to rise, but felt
Oppressed as if with sleep, and Azraeel's sword
Waved o'er his head. He never rose again.   140

CANTO II.

EL KHIDR AND ILYAHS.

WHEN King Iskender took the central path,
El Khadir and his brother chanced to meet,
And they determined not to part again.
Down, down they rode; the winding pathway led
Still down. At length they drew their horses'reins, 145
In terror, for they trod the very brink
Of such a precipice as ne'er before
Had mortal seen. The brothers sprang to earth,
And Ilyash leaning o'er the cliff, perceived
The Fountain they were seeking. "Look, El Khidr, 150
The Fountain is below us!" he exclaimed.
El Khadir looked, and seized a heavy stone,

And cast it down. A moment, and the plunge
Denoted at what fearful depth below,
The Fountain lay. El Khadir then exclaimed: 155
"Ilyahs, it must be useless to attempt
To reach the Fountain. We must strive to find
Some other pathway. See how deep and smooth
The precipice below us!" — But at this,
His brother interrupted him. "Behold!   160
One way there is, it seems the only way:
God and the Prophets aid me!" Then he gazed
Again unshrinking down the deep abyss.
"Farewell, El Khadir!" And the fearless youth
Sprang from the precipice. El Khadir looked   165
In grief and wonder down; but Ilyahs plunged
Deep in the sacred Fount. He rose again,
And drank until he felt Israhfeel's Trump
Alone had power to end his fated life;
And power miraculous that hour was his.   170
   El Khadir dared not seek the camp again,
Alone to meet his father, and he strove
With cautious steps to find a path below,
And ascertain his brother's life or death.
He soon perceived how hopeless was the task,   175
And tried to reascend, but tried in vain.
Descend he could not. To the rocks he clung,
For life and death: he did not dare to move,
And every moment he perceived his hold
Was weaker, and the rocks had cut his hands.   180
His wounded hands refused to hold the rocks,
And underneath his feet the stones gave way.
   "Ilyahs!" El Khadir cried, "thy fate is mine,
And even Azraeel cannot part us now!"

With that he fell. The Fountain that he sought   185
Received him; and on rising up, he drank
The water that Iskender might not taste.
Then Ilyahs, where he stood upon a rock,
Called him, and side by side the brothers stood,
O'ercome with holy awe. They soon perceived   190
A path by which to scale the cliff above.
But as they went to reascend, behold!
The cavern roof above is cleft in twain,
And on them shines a flood of heavenly light.

    Israhfeel stood before them: "Be it yours,   195
To range the earth and sea, and save the lives
Of true Believers. Power miraculous
Is granted you, O Prophets! More than this,
Whene'er you need their aid, Believing Jinn
Shall serve you. Quit the cavern, and return   200
To King Iskender's army, and protect
Your father till he dies."
                  The angel spoke,
And vanished. Lost in thought the brothers climbed
The precipice, and mounting each his mare,
In silence through the awful cave they rode,   205
And near the entrance they Iskender met,
And rode with him to join their friends again.

    Then a great earthquake shook, and closed for aye,
The cave that held the Fountain, from mankind.

END OF THE FOURTH BOOK.

BOOK THE FIFTH.

THE DAUGHTER OF IBLEES.

ARGUMENT.

I   Consultation between Iblees and his sons. Balkees sent to the earth to tempt Hasan. He converts aud marries her. Death of Hasan. Balkees departs to Jinneestahn.

II.   Balkees follows the chain of Kahf, in search of Jinneestahn. Monsters of the mountains and the sea. She arrives at the Sea of Darkness. Her meeting with Soht. She retraces her flight.

III.   Iblees and his sons pursue Balkees. She falls mortally wounded on the Coral Reef of Jinneestahn. Her interview with Ed-Dimiryaht. Her death. Battle of the Jinn at Damascus. Total defeat of Iblees.

CANTO I.

BALKEES AND HASAN,

Now must we leave the splendour of the Heavens,
And the blue glory of the aerial sea,
And all the life and beauty of the earth,
And all the dazzling light of Jinnestahn,

And seek again the awful Seventh Earth,   5
Now tenfold more accursed than of yore,
Since Iblees and his troops their empire raised
In its drear realms of horror. Iblees knew
His power was broken, and despairingly
Consulted with his two surviving sons,   10
And laid his plans before them.
                                "We may fight,"
Said Teer at length, "in vain against the King
Who rules the gorgeous realms of Jinneestahn:
But we may hope by subtlety and craft,
To lead the instructors of mankind astray: •   15
And chief among them now, as I have learned,
Is Hasan of Damascus, who can trace
His ancestry to Ahssaf. He has wrought
More harm to us than twenty meaner foes;
For many trust in Allah, whom he led   20
Away from us."
                    With gloomy frown the Chief
Heard these unwelcome tidings from his son:
He sat awhile in silence; then exclaimed,
"Call here my daughter Balkees! [74] I have sought
To teach her ill was good, and good was ill;   25
Yet has she never yet essayed to lead
A soul away from Allah. Let her go,
And snare this great opponent in her toils!"
    "Beware!" replied the all-deceiver Soht,
"Lest she herself should yield to Hasan's power: 30
For those who are not yet defiled with sin,
Shrink back in terror when they meet it first,
And if they chance to fall in virtue's path,
They follow virtue, and adore the God

Whom we abhor, and utterly renounce!"   35
  Yet darker grew the frown on Iblees' brow,
As Soht was speaking. "Woe to you!" he cried.
Think you your sister Balkees e'er would stoop
To Allah or to virtue, or would fear
To plunge herself in sin, or e'er permit   40
Our foes to lead her mind so far astray,
That she should bow to our ancestral foe!
She is not so unworthy of her race!"
  "But", answered Soht, "I say again, Beware". —
Iblees would hear no more, and thundered forth,   45
"Be silent! She shall go without a guard,
And by her single unassisted power
Shall conquer Hasan, for I will not send
A single messenger to all the town
Where Hasan dwells, save Balkees. She shall stay   50
For years, if need exists, among the men
Who reverence Hasan, till she treads him down,
Body and soul alike, beneath her feet!"
  He ceased, and Soht a moment left the hall,
Returning soon with Balkees. "Leave me now,"   55
Said Iblees to his sons, and they obeyed.
  "Go, Balkees, to Damascus. There resides
A Sheykh named Hasan, such a foe to us,
That Allah, our remorseless enemy,
Views him with favour. Hasan leads away   60
Our firmest friends to Allah. You must strive
For years if need be till the youthful sage
Abandons God, and uses all his power
To lead to me again the craven souls
Whom he has led to Allah. Balkees, go,   65
And be my holiest blessings on your head.

May none of all the Jinn who worship me,
Sink deeper in the yawning gulfs of Hell!"
   Then Iblees tought her where to seek her foe,
And Balkees to the highest earth arose.   70
The lessons taught her on the Seventh Earth
Were to love sin and darkness, and abhor
All virtue and religion. But she knew
By practice nought of either; for before
She ne'er was sent above the Seventh Earth.   75
   High o'er the First Earth the Jinneeyeh rose,
And hung awhile in motionless surprise.
Was this the land whose people she must hate,
And whose Creator was her deadliest foe?
A land more beautiful ten thousand times   80
Than was the Seventh Earth, though far below
The dazzling splendour of the Seven Heavens,
Or Jinneestahn, whose very air is Light?
Well might the truth of Nature find its way
Deep in her heart!
                "Let Allah be my God!"   85
She thought within herself, "my father's power
Could never make a world as bright as this.
O surely Iblees cannot be a god,
Or wherefore is the Seventh Earth his home?
I will not tempt mankind, until I know   90
Why Iblees hates the human race, and God.
How buoyant and how pure the air of earth!
The sky is brilliant blue, not black like ours,
And the green verdure, springing everywhere,
Is all unknown upon the Seventh Earth.   95
O wise Creator, whomsoe'er thou art,
Lead me to know thee, and I'll worship thee,

And practise thy commands!"

                   Thus Balkees spoke,
And soaring far above the highest Earth,
She found that she had reached the aerial sea,   100
Whose waves of blue, illimitable air,
Flow pure and cold between the earth and heaven.
Awhile she revelled in her new-felt life,
Then sinking nearer to the earth, she flew
Until she reached Damascus, where she hoped   105
To find the virtuous Hasan, and from him
To learn the truth that she was sent to quell.

   At length she found the youth. Around him stood
A crowd of eager listeners, as he told
How wonderful was Allah's boundless love,   110
And how no sinner ever yet was lost,
Beyond all hope of pardon.

                      "God be praised!"
Cried Hasan, with a look of lofty joy:
"Iblees himself at length shall bow to Him!"

   Then Balkees took a human form, and stood   115
Among the attentive crowd, and heard with joy
The praise of God and virtue. Every word
Sank like an arrow barbed with quenchless light,
Deep in her heart: and like a nightmare dream,
Her evil learning vanished from her mind.   120

   Hasan at length departed to his home,
And Balkees followed. "Master!" she exclaimed,
"May one who ever has been reared in sin,
Learn truth from thee that may dispel the shades
Of darkness, that she long has learned to think   125
Was really truth?"

               "My mission is from God,"

Replied the Sheykh, "to teach his truth to all
Who know it not."
                      Emboldened by his words,
She asked the truth about Suleymahn's reign,
And of the race of the Believing Jinn,   130
And the great Wezeer Ahssaf.   Then she asked
How Iblees fell, and wherefore he was doomed
To dwell upon the accursed Seventh Earth,
And wherefore he detested God and man?
    Hasan replied to everything she asked;   135
Then she stood up revealed, and spoke: "Alas!
Will Iblees ever be restored to Heaven,
And can his children ever come to God,
If so they wish? Then hope perchance there is,
For Iblees' daughter, Balkees, whom you see!   140
O willingly to Allah would I bow,
But rather than desert my evil race,
Would share, their punishment, if thus I hoped
To lighten it for them."
                          Then Hasan sprang
In momentary terror, from his seat.   145
"O daughter of the Accursed, dare you swear
That you will never strive to injure men,
Or thwart the plans of Allah?"
                                Thus he spoke.
And named the Name on which she was to swear,
And fearlessly she took the awful oath.   150
    "Let me," said Balkees, "daily learn from you,
The truths that all my evil race oppose.
Why should I not, Jinneeyeh as I am,
Learn truths from you that ne'er I knew before?"
"So be it!" Hasan answered. As he spoke,   155

His pupil Balkees vanished from his sight.
Each day to Hasan Balkees came to learn
The holiest teachings e'er revealed to men;
And e'en when Hasan deemed himself alone,
She still watched o'er him, visible to none.   160
Nor was it long before a mutual love
Sprang up between them; and at length it chanced,
One morning Hasan in his house alone,
Was reading in an ancient Hebrew book,
Of King Suleymahn's glory, and his love   165
For Bilkees, Queen of Seba; and the name
Recalled his pupil Balkees, and he felt
That she was now his all in all of life,
Although she sprang from such an evil race.
He closed the book, and half unconsciously   170
Pronounced her name, and instantly he saw
Balkees before him. "I have not confessed,"
She said, "that Iblees sent me to destroy
The race of men; but nature's beauty first
Awoke the love of Allah in my heart.   175
Hasan, I came to harm you most of all,
But I will never, never seek again
The accursed Seventh Earth; but here will dwell,
And night and day will guard you from your foes!"
She knelt before him humbly. He replied,   180
"Why, Balkees, should I blame you for a sin
Which never was committed? I rejoice
To know that while I live a power like yours
Is watching over me; but answer me,
Think you that blood and flame can e'er unite?"   185
"Unite!" cried Balkees, as she read his heart;
"Did Seyf El Mulook [15] wed a human bride?

Say, was Esh-Shems a woman? Tell me who
Of all the ancient heroes, was content
With human wives? A fourth of flame was mixed   190
E'en with the blood that flowed in Bilkees' veins:
Yet Bilkees was Suleymahn's favourite wife!"

She ceased, and bent her eyes upon the ground,
And Hasan took her gently by the hand,
And answered, "Balkees, since I knew you first,   195
I grew to love you, but I would not ask
That you should ever link your fate with mine,
For you would quickly lose me. Know you not,
How few among us live a hundred years?"

"'Tis true," said Balkees, "but we part no more,   200
Till Azraeel parts us, when if I survive,
I'll seek for Jinneestahn in Eastern Kahf,
And there await the Second Trumpet-Blast,
That reunites all friends for evermore.
And though your efforts in the cause of Truth,   205
Have much destroyed your health, yet I am sent,
To soothe your few remaining days on earth,
By Allah as I think; and I implore
That since you love me, I may be your bride".

"I love thee, Balkees, love thee all too well,   210
And therefore would not wed thee, for thou knowst
The great uncertainty of human life:
Yet thou hast spoken of thine own free will:
Hear then the vows that I will make to thee.

"By the stars that gleam in the distant sky,   215
Whose number baffles the keenest eye:
By the Essence that rules the wondrous Whole,
By thy Race of Flame, and thy deathless soul,

By the verdant earth, and the viewless air,
And the water that wanders everywhere,   220
I swear to love thee eternally.
The stars may darken and fade and die,
But those united by love like ours,
Defy the strongest of Nature's powers;
And nothing in heaven or earth has might,   225
To sever the souls that love aright!"

As Hasan spoke, an aged Sheykh who taught
His wisdom to the youth, had opened wide
The door, and stood awhile in mute surprise,
Till Hasan called him, and the story told   230
Of Balkees and their love. They sent at once,
And called the Kahdee and the witnesses,
And Balkees stood by Hasan as his wife,
And old Abd-Allah, Hasan's master, blessed
Hasan and Balkees.
                    Long they dwelt in peace,   235
All unmolested by the Evil Jinn,
Till Balkees, with a mother's pride and joy,
Placed her first infant in its father's arms.
But Hasan viewed it with a mournful smile.
"Balkees", said Hasan, "let my son be sent   240
To old Abd-Allah, who can teach him all
That I myself learned from him years ago.
Such is my wish, revere it as my last;
For now my health is utterly destroyed,
And I must pay for wisdom by a death   245
That might not come so early, had I cast
My knowledge to the winds, and lived as those
Who nothing care for fame, and do not seek
To leave the world the better for their lives."
She fell before him weeping; but at last   250

She roused herself, and asked : "But know you not
Some drug or spell that might prolong your life?"
"None!" answered Hasan; but as Hasan spoke,
Abd-Allah entered, and perceived at once
That Hasan's valued life was near its close.   255
"Give me your infant son," Abd-Allah cried,
"And I will teach him wisdom, and will make
The child the wisest Sheykh in all the earth!"
Balkees, absorbed in Hasan's certain doom,
Then placed the child in old Abd-Allah's arms.   260
"Can you save Hasan from impending fate?"
She asked. Abd-Allah answered, "He must die!
I fear no human aid can save him now,
And you, Jinneeyeh, know no healing spells.
The spells you learned upon the Seventh Earth,   265
Might blast like lightning, but could never heal."
"Then will I watch beside him till his death,"
Balkees replied, "and afterwards will fly
To ask the King of the Believing Jinn
To guard my son from Iblees and his troops."   270
She ceased, and looked at Hasan, who had fallen
Upon the ground beside her. Balkees knelt,
And upon Hasan's heart she laid her hand,
And listened for his breathing, but in vain.
Hasan was dead, and with a bitter cry,   275
Balkees sank down upon him in her grief.
    Abd-Allah tried to soothe her, and at length
She rose, and thanked him: then with wilder grief,
She cried, "Abd-Allah, I can never bear
To see my Hasan buried. Let me go,   280
And in my efforts to preserve his child,
Attempt to cast away my load of grief.

Let him be buried, but O do not ask
That I should stay to view it! I will fly
To ask the King of Jinneestahn to guard   285
My infant."
           "Such a journey, I perceive,
Will cost your life," Abd-Allah made reply,
"For you must die beneath your father's hand:
But Ed-Dimiryaht will protect your son."
The grief of Balkees was at once dispelled.   290
"Thank God that death awaits me!" she exclaimed.
"When this last task is over, I shall meet
My Hasan, and to part, O nevermore!"
She vanished, and Abd-Allah laid to rest
The lifeless corpse of Hasan, and he vowed   295
That Hasan's son in wisdom should surpass
Himself and Hasan, and he kept his vow,
For, for dead Hasan's sake, he reared the boy
So well, that never lived a wiser Sheykh,
Than was Abd-Allah's pupil, Hasan's son,   300
Who, by his piety and wisdom, gained
A knowledge of the Name of God, inscribed
By God himself upon Suleymahn's Seal.

CANTO II.

MOUNT KAHF.

When Balkees vanished from Abd-Allah's sight,
She knew not where to seek for Jinneestahn,   305
But only knew it bordered on Mount Kahf,

10

So she resolved that she would fly within
The mighty chain of Kahf, until she reached
King Ed-Dimiryaht's realms. She bent her way
North-east with lightning swiftness. Soon she left   310
The dwellings of mankind behind her far,
And everywhere a desert vast appeared,
And passing that, she flew across a sea
Which shone like silver, but which never moved,
And in its moveless stillness, most was like   315
The Fiery Sea [76] that forms the core of earth,
Revealed to Psychometric gaze alone;
But this was silver-bright, not fiery red,
Nor subject to the storms that shake the earth,
And formed of mercury [77] untarnished, pure,   320
And not a molten mass of glowing rock,
As is the inward sea. She swiftly passed
The Sea of Mercury, when she beheld
A huge black mountain of enormous height;
And when she viewed it closer, she perceived   325
The mountain was composed of solid iron.
No earthly verdure clothed its dusky sides:
The rivers flowing through its vales, were tinged
As red as blood with metal; and the trees
Upon the Iron Mountain bore for leaves   330
Falchions of shining steel; their buds were spears,
And an armed warrior was the perfect fruit.
So shall that crop of warriors still increase
Until Iskender's barrier is removed, [78]
And Gog and Magog shall o'errun the earth,   335
And lead these iron warriors on to war.
    Above the Iron Mountain Balkees rose,
And saw beyond the gloomy Outer Sea,

Then rising far above the storms, she saw
The brilliant emerald mountain, Kahf, whose peaks 340
Were lost amid the spotless blue of heaven.
  No speck of snow can touch the peaks of Kahf,
But in the centre of the ocean rose
An island with a lofty mountain-peak,
That seemed to rival e'en the height of Kahf.   345
A gloomy precipice the mountain formed:
Its head was crowned with everlasting snows.
Three hundred miles one jutting granite rock,
Projecting from the loftier mountain's side,
Measured from base to summit. It was seamed,   350
And split by fissures. Many a crag had fallen,
And splintered as it fell, the cliff below.
Above it rose the mountain, well defined,
O'ertopping all the storms, its mighty peaks
Gleaming distinct. And as she gazed, a rock   355
Dislodged from that enormous mountain's side,
Rushed downwards, and the echoes loud and long
Repeated followed. But the rock itself,
Had rolled from near the summit of the hill,
And numerous other stones pursued it down.   360
Thundering it fell, now leaping many a mile,
Now shivering all to fragments some vast rock
That in the mountain fixed, beyond the rest,
Had stood. A lake was under it; it fell
Amid the waters, which recoiled, and swept   365
Far o'er the neighbouring snows, the splintered ice
Upheaved around in many a wall of glass.
At length it reached the granite rock below,
And fell upon the summit with a sound
That rang from Kahf to Kahf. The wall of rock   370

Was split to pieces, while the falling stone
Leaped far into the sea, which upward rushed,
And swept the stones away; and when it sank,
No traces of the granite rock remained.
    "If I could reach the highest peaks of Kahf,"   375
Said Balkees to herself, "I might behold   -
All regions of the earth, from Kahf to Kahf,
And perhaps the glorious land of Jinneestahn."
    Up the Green Mountain's sides she bent her way,
But after she had flown a thousand miles,   380
She could not then behold the mountain-peaks,
So judged it best to fly within the mount,
For as she knew the mountain was a ring,
She could not fail in finding Jinneestahn.
But who can know the things which God conceals? 385
Instead of turning to the East, she turned
Towards the Sea of Darkness in the West.
    She saw the islands of the Outer Sea,
Where roam the mightiest monsters of the earth.
Enormous serpents wind their slimy coils [70]   390
Amid the forests, and the elephant
Is but a morsel to its fearful foes,
Who swallow one alive, and closely wind
Around a mighty tree, and crush to pulp
The prey devoured before; but they themselves,   395
The Seemurgh and the Rukh destroy for food.
May Allah guard the ships that tempt the deep,
From monsters like the fearful fish that swim
Around the islands of the Outer Sea!
The hugest ship that ever yet was built,   400
The very least could crush within its jaws!
    Balkees, whose wings were weary, caught a Rukh,

And sprang npon its neck, and seized its head,
And forced it to obey her, and the bird
Flew swiftly in its terror to the spot,   405
Where flows the Sea of Darkness. Balkees saw
The gathering night before, and left the Rukh,
And hovered ou the borders of the gloom,
Unknowing whether she had best advance,
Or by the pathway that she came, return.   410
At length amid the darkness, she perceived
A Jinnee flying swiftly. Soon she knew
Her brother Soht, and then she felt afraid.
"Ah sister!" he exclaimed, "your work is done?
Is Hasan's soul our father's? Do you wish,   415
Before descending to the Seventh Earth,
To view the realms of Kahf? I wish you joy;
For this is Iblees' earthly home amid
A land of welcome darkness. He is here,
And will receive you with a father's pride.   420
My brother Teer is with us. We design
Again to rush on Jinneestahn, which lies
Far distant from our realms, in Eastern Kahf."
With terror and abhorrence Balkees heard,
And turned away from Soht, who instantly   425
Perceived she did not worship Iblees now:
So rushing to her, in an altered tone,
Which well that false deceiver could assume,
He cried, "Believe not, Balkees, what I spoke.
I said it but to try you; for I knew,   430
When Iblees sent you forth into the world,
That you would shortly turn away from him.
Although I dare not openly proclaim
My faith in Allah, yet I work for him,

And therefore oft oppose my father's plans."   435
Balkees was quite deluded with his words,
And thinking he would sympathise with her,
She told him all her story. As she spoke,
She saw how stern and angry was his look;
But when she ceased, he answered, "You betrayed 440
Our cause, and ne'er shall fly to Jinneestahn,
For we will follow, and will drag you here,
And when we've slain your child before your eyes,
You die by dreadful tortures!"
                                Balkees heard
His threat in terror, and she rushed away,   445
And fearfully pursued the backward path,
From which she swerved no more. She longed to seize
Another Rukh; but none were near her now,
And wearied as she was, she could not hope
To overtake the bird, if one she saw.   450
Nor had she time, for well she knew that Soht
Would soon pursue her with a numerous host.
She thought not now of all the wondrous sights
That lay around her, fresh at every stroke:
She only hoped to fly to Jinneestahn,   455
Before her foes could intercept her path.

CANTO III.

THE DEATH OF BALKEES.

Soht swiftly to the Throne of Iblees flew,
And Teer and Iblees, when they heard his tale,

Sprang to their feet in wráth. They seized their spears,
And calling forth two hundred swift-winged Jinn,   460
Rushed after Balkees. Iblees gave command:
"Pursue my daughter till you see afar
The land of Jinneestahn, but strike her not,
Until she thinks that every danger's o'er:
Then hurl your spears, and pierce her to the heart. 465
But tremble if you overtake her not,
Or if she safely reaches Jinneestahn,
For I will slay you all. Pursue her close,
But do not let her see us, till we strike
A vile Jinneeych faithless to our cause!"   470
    Aloug the range of Kahf the squadron flew,
Till Balkees was before them. They delayed,
Attempting but to keep her in their sight,
As Iblees had commanded. Oft she turned,
And fearful looked behind her, but her foes   475
She saw not, and her hopes again revived.
She dared not stay, but flew with all her speed,
Along the mountain, whose stupendous peaks
Rose on her left, aloft she knew not where.
    At length she neared the bounds of Jinneestahn,   480
When Iblees gave the order, "Hurl your spears!"
Then Balkees turned in fear, and saw the foes
Whose spears were hurtling round her. Far before,
She saw the quenchless light of Jinneestahn,
And rising o'er the stormy Outer Sea,   485
She flew with doubled swiftness to her goal,
For if she could attain the Coral Reef,
Which formed the boundary of the calmer sea,
She knew that she was safe. Her vengeful foes
Cast their sharp spears around, but touched her not, 490

And Iblees, Teer, and Soht alone retained
The spears they bore. They saw the guards were roused,
And charging on them; but to fiends like those,
Revenge was more than safety. Teer and Soht
Now aimed their spears at Balkees, but in vain.   495
One flew above her shoulder; one was hurled
Through her long plumes; but neither touched the skin.
Balkees was now above the Coral Reef,
When Iblees, foaming with despair and rage,
Cast the last spear; it pierced his daughter's side;   500
One last convulsive stroke she smote the air,
Faltered; and swooning fell upon the Reef;
While Iblees, and his band of Evil Jinn,
Fled from the guards, who cared not to pursue.
    They raised the dying Balkees from the ground, 505
But found the wound was mortal. Balkees woke,
And looked bewildered at the Jinnee guards;
Then she remembered all, and faintly spoke:
"Heed not my wound, for I am doomed to die,
But call King Ed-Dimiryaht to my side,   510
For I would speak to him before my death."
    They cast some incense on a censer near, [35]
And called on Ed-Dimiryaht. He appeared
Before them in an instant. "Know, O King,"
The Jinnee who had summoned him began,   515
"A squadron of the Evil Jinn pursued,
E'en to the boundary line of Jinneestahn,
This weak, unarmed Jinneeyeh; and at length,
They hurled a spear that pierced her. She demands
To speak with you yourself before her death."   520
    King Ed-Dimiryaht knelt by Balkees' side,
And laid his hand upon the fatal spear,

But did not dare to move it.
               "I have come,"
Said Balkees, "from Damascus. I was sent
To tempt its people to renounce their God;   525
For I am Balkees, Iblees' youngest child.
But Hasan was a Sheykh, my father's foe,
Who taught me to desert my evil course,
And I became his bride. My son I left
With wise Abd-Allah; and at Hasan's death,   530
I came to ask you to protect my child,
And in my ignorance, I chanced to fly
Towards the realms of Iblees. Soht deceived,
And made me tell him all that I had done,
And Iblees and his sons pursued me here,   535
And Iblees' spear has wounded me to death."
    "Where dwells Abd-Allah, for I know him not?"
Responded Ed-Dimiryaht.
                  Balkees spoke
More faintly as she answered: "He delights
To rear in wisdom, and in innocence,   540
The children of the Sheykhs; and he it was,
Who taught my husband Hasan all he knew ;
And Hasan, as you may perchance have heard,
Could trace his noble ancestry to one
Who once, O Ed-Dimiryaht, was your friend,   545
Ahssaf, Barkhiya's son. Abd-Allah dwells
A league without the city's eastern gate.
But O, protect him now !"
                The King replied,
"By the dread spell on King Suleymahn's Seal,
I swear to guard your child from Evil Jinn,   550
And guard Abd-Allah also from his foes."

Then, turning to a guard: "You hear her words:
Send off immediately twelve thousand Jinn,
And bid them guard Abd Allah. I will come,
And quickly join the troops."

He spoke, and turned   555
Again to Balkees, but she could not speak,
And the spear-shaft was flaming. Soon it fell,
A heap of ashes, but the head remained,
Although exposed to more than furnace heat.
He knew to draw the head was instant death,   560
And as he anxiously surveyed the steel,
He saw it glowing with a dusky red,
An ominous hue, which instantly was changed
To brilliant scarlet, for the head of steel,
Was heated to the utmost. Balkees sank   565
Expiring on the reef. The glowing steel
Dripped melting from the wound; a rush of flames
Succeeded, and they coiled themselves around
The prostrate form of Balkees. Soon they cleared:
Where she had lain, a heap of ashes lay;   570
And she and Hasan met again with joy,
Before the bridge Siraht, which bore their weight,
And led them to a happier land than earth,
Where those who meet in friendship shall not part;
And both were well repaid for all the woe   575
They suffered, while they dwelt upon the earth.

    When Ed-Dimiryaht saw his suppliant dead,
He hastened to Damascus, where he found
His troops assembled round Abd-Allah's house.
But Iblees gathered all the Evil Jinn,   580
And led them to Damascus, where they met
The troops of Ed-Dimiryaht. Long they fought,

Till the Believing Jinn dispersed their foes,
And though outnumbered by the Evil Jinn,
Slew thousands; and among them Soht was slain   585
By Ed-Dimiryaht. Teer and Iblees fled,
Nor dared again Abd-Allah to assail,
And when at length they reached their own abodes,
They found with helpless rage how few were left.
    Iblees had boasted he would fight with God,   590
And hurl him from his Throne; but where were now
The angels and the Jinn who were to join
The son of Jarjarees? Of angels few
Had ever joined him, of the Jinn a third
Had turned against him, while of those who joined 595
The self-elected monarch of the Jinn,
Had millions perished in the constant wars
That he himself had forced on Jinneestahn:
Or by the shooting stars that angels cast
Against the troops of Iblees, when they fly   600
Beneath the lowest Heaven, to hear their words.
    Yet still his pride upheld him, though subdued,
And all his projects scattered to the winds.
'Twas not the pride that fills a man whom God
Has set a goal of virtue or of fame   605
To reach; whose life is charmed until his work
Is ended; but the evil, envious pride
That leads a man who knows his words are false,
To speak against a nobler man than he,
And call him vile; and this consuming pride   610
Was one of Iblees' greatest earthly pains:
Nor till that pride was broken, could he hope
For pardon from the God he had renounced.

END OF THE FIFTH BOOK.

BOOK THE SIXTH.

THE CLOSE OF A CYCLE.

ARGUMENT.

I. Signs of the End. Conversation between Ed-Dimiryaht and Sahleh. Arrival of El Khidr and Ilyahs. Iblees warned for the last time. Ed-Dimiryaht's address to his subjects. Israhfeel sounds the First Trumpet. The convulsions of Nature which follow. Ruin of Jinneestahn. Courage of the Jinn. The Second Trumpet sounded. The universal death which succeeds. Resurrection of the Archangels.

II. The Third Trumpet sounded. The General Resurrection. The passage of the Sirabt. Meeting of Ed-Dimiryaht and Dahish. The Fall of the Bridge. Condition of Iblees and his followers. Anticipations of the Future.

III. Repentance of Dahsim and El Aawar. Ed-Dimiryaht sent to deliver them. Eesa and the Jinneeyehs. Repentance of Soht and Teer, and ultimately of Iblees. Annihilation of Jahennem.

IV. The glorified Universe. The leaders of their races. Conclusion.

CANTO I.

THE TRUMPET OF ISRAHFEEL.

To those who live until the Second Blast
The Trumpet-Angel sounds, how rapidly

Do years and centuries appear to move!
Save Ed-Dimiryaht, all the Jinn are barred
From Heaven; and kingdoms rise and fall on earth; 5
And ceaselessly throughout all time, the Jinn
Work to promote the weal or woe of men,
According to the masters that they serve.
But now at length the last great signs appear,
Such as the seers in ages past foretold 10
The Blast of Consternation should precede.
The ancient prophecies were all fulfilled,
And Ed-Dimiryaht on his palace stood,
And as he looked towards the human world,
He saw that all was calm.
　　　　　　　　　　"If so it be," 15
He prayed within himself, "if 'tis the End,
O Allah, grant me once again to warn
The Evil Jinn upon the Seventh Earth!"
　　Then he an Efreet called: "Bid Sahleh here!"
And still he gazed around him, for the day 20
Was calm, a calm like that before a storm!
Calm was that day, calm even for Jinneestahn:
The rainbow networks high above his head,
Flung down their shadows motionless around.
The suns shone down upon the moveless sea, 25
And like a sea of glass, the sea reflects
The rainbows and the suns. He stood and gazed,
Till from the ocean depths King Sahleh rose;
And Ed-Dimiryaht, when he joined him, led
The Diver to his palace.
　　　　　　　　　　"Hast thou seen, 30
O Sahleh, that the world draws near its end?
I would assemble all my subjects here,

And warn them of the Trumpet, and the Bridge
That lies across Jahennem."
                              "Let me go."
King Sahleh cried, "to call the Diving Jinn,   35
And lead them to your palace."
                         • "Hear me out.
If as I think, the End indeed is near,
Why should the knowledge be witheld from us,
Who are resisted Iblees? Stay with me,
For we shall be acquainted with the truth,   40
Before the Blast of Consternation sounds,
Which none but true believers hear unmoved." ·
    Thus they; but e'en as Ed-Dimiryaht speaks'
El Khadir mounts with Ilyahs in a car
Composed of clouds, which bears them swift away   45
To Ed-Dimiryaht's palace, while it veils
The splendour of Joharahbahd, which not
The eyes of even Prophets great as those,
Could ever bear. Enveloped in the clouds,
The Prophets sank before the King they sought.   50
"O Ed-Dimiryaht, hear us! Even now,
Israhfeel stands prepared to sound the Blast
Of Consternation. To the Seventh Earth
Descend, and warn the Jinn that Iblees rules:
Then call your subjects to Joharahbahd,   55
And bid them hear the Trumpet-Blast unmoved,
When mountains crumble."
                          "Prophets, I obey!"
King Ed-Dimiryaht answered, as the cloud
Again departed to the World of Men.
    "Go, Sahleh, summon here the Diving Jinn!"   60
He cried, "and bid Marjahneh instantly

Assemble all my subjects! They shall hear
The Trumpet-Blast, and quail not at the sound!"
   King Sahleb left him.   Ed-Dimiryaht struck
The floor, and clove a pathway for himself,   65
And ever plunging deeper, instantly
He reached the Seventh Earth, and stood again
In Iblees' hall, among the Evil Jinn,
Who feared the Trumpet, and in council sat.
How changed were they! How altered was the hall! 70
How hideous were their forms and features now!
How gloomy and how dreadful was the hall!
The floor was strewn with ashes soaked in blood,
And all the walls were black with blood, and smeared
With hideous paintings of more dreadful deeds.   75
   Before the fiends King Ed-Dimiryaht stood,
Still beautiful in his eternal youth,
And none among them knew him, but they thought
That Azraeel came to summon them.   He spoke:
"Israhfeel's Trumpet is upraised! He waits   80
His Master's word to sound.   Repent ye all!
I come to warn you of the bridge Siraht,
And of the pit of flame that roars below.
Ye may perchance escape Jahennem yet:
O hear my warning! Ha, ye know me not?   85
Zelemboor's son am I; and now the King
Of Jinneestahn."
            Then Iblees cried in wrath:
"O ye who serve the son of Jarjarees,
Assemble round my throne! Our doom is fixed.
And, Ed-Dimiryaht, coward as you are,   90
You dare to threaten those who fear not God!
Begone, nor venture to disturb us more!"

Around his throne his evil legions thronged,
And Ed-Dimiryaht spoke again. "Reflect!
The Trumpet has not sounded. Ye may hope
For pardon yet. Till forty years have passed,
We do not meet again. But Iblees say,
Where is your daughter Balkees whom you slew,
Because she did not dare contend with God,
And tried in vain to escape you, knowing not   100
The way to Jinneestahn? And ye who stand
Around the accursed son of Jarjarees,
Have ye forgot the innocence of heaven,
Its beauty and its love?"
                                Enraged they heard,
And storms of fear, remorse, and hatred rushed   105
Across their hideous features.
                                "Woe to you!"
At length said Ed-Dimiryaht, "all in vain
I came to warn you of your woe deserved,
And I must leave you to your awful doom!"
    But no one chose to answer him again,   110
And to Joharahbahd the King returned,
And found his subjects waiting his commands.
    He laid his crown and sceptre on his throne.
"Alas!" he said, "my warnings were in vain,
For e'en the Blast of Consternation, ne'er   115
Has power to rouse the Unbelieving Jinn.
Believers, ye obeyed me as your King,
But now it matters not. Israhfeel stands
Prepared to sound the Consternation Blast,
Which none but true believers hear unmoved.   120
Why should we fear the Trumpet? We are true,
And kept aloof from Iblees and his troops.

Our duties upon earth are ended now,
But greater glories wait us than we see
In e'en our gorgeous land of Jinneestahn.   125
I would not have you hear the Blast unwarned,
Though when it sounds, we know no cause for fear."
  Then all arose to applaud their noble King,
But o'er their shouts there pealed a fearful sound,
The Blast of Consternation.
                        "Lo, ye hear,"   130
King Ed-Dimiryaht cried, "the Trumpet peal.
Come, quit the palace with me, and behold
The devastation that the Trump of Doom
Is causing!"
              From the palace swift they flew,
And still the Blast of Consternation pealed.   135
Where are the glories of Joharahbahd?
The rainbows, suns, and moons, and belts are gone.
The stars have fallen; and though securely stands
The mountain Kahf, all other mountains fall
In heaps of dust. The cities of the earth,   140
Are laid in ruins; and Joharahbahd
Quakes to its firm foundations, and they hear
Above the ruin, still the Trumpet peal.
The sea retreats beyond the Coral Reef,
Then swelling up in one prodigious wave,   145
Like those that follow earthquakes on the coast,
Breaks down the Coral Reef, and Amberabahd
Is torn from its foundations; then the wave
With water's slow and treacherous fury, rakes
The valley Jinneestahn from end to end;   150
And every palace in Joharahbahd
Is levelled with the ground. The sea retreats,

And leaves the scene of desolation bare,
Save where the bright Joharahbahd had stood,
Where still remain some broken blocks of gems.
  At length the Trumpet's thunder died away,
And on the ruins of Joharahbahd,
King Ed-Dimiryaht sank: "O friends," he cried,
"Our work is done; may God receive our souls!
We soon shall hear the second peal and sleep   160
In peace for forty years, until the Blast
Of Resurrection shall restore our lives:
And Heaven, more bright than e'en Joharahbahd,
Shall shine when falls Jahennem, brighter yet."
Thus spoke the King, and when they heard his words, 165
No more they feared the Consternation-Blast,
Nor mourned their cities utterly destroyed.
  Then cried Marjahneh, "Wherefore should we fear
The Bridge Siraht, although that awful Bridge
Across Jahennem's flaming gulf is placed?   170
'Tis sharper than the Sword of Jarjarees.
And finer than a hair, and girt about
With thorns and briars. This Bridge we all must tread,
Before we reach the gates of Paradise.
Our wings are useless there, for none may pass   175
That gulf by flight, but by the Bridge alone.
Fear not the Bridge of Breadth!"

                              "That will we not!"
The Jinn exclaimed; and now Meyniooneh rose.
  "I neither fear the Bridge, nor fear the Trump,
That soon shall sound; and this I owe to thee,   180
O Father, who amid the accursed hosts,
Stood firm beside my mother, nor would deign
To bow before the son of Jarjarees.

Well I deserve my name of Fortunate![34]
For all," —
                     But now the Trumpet's sound was heard, 185
And every voice in Heaven or Earth was hushed,
For Azraeel waved his Sword through all the worlds,
And every living thing that instant died.
Iblees and all his troops, who struck with fear
Had desperately resolved to fight with God,   190
Fell lifeless ere they left the Seventh Earth.
Then Azraeel o'er the Archangels shook his Sword,
And, as Israhfeel let the Trumpet fall,
And sank expiring at his feet, he shook
The Sword above himself. He sank and died,   195
But that dread Sword became a golden Key.
    The glories of the earth and Jinneestahn,
Are gone for ever. Of Joharahbahd,
Nought now remained but heaps of precious stones,
And ashes. Ilyahs and El Khidr might gaze   200
With safety on the ruins, did they live,
Undazzled by the Jewel City's glare.
All earthly splendour is reduced to dust,
And God alone survives the Trumpet-Blast.
    For forty years this universal death   205
Must last; and then the Resurrection-Blast
Will raise the death to judgment. Allah speaks,
And the Archangels rise upon their feet.
Israhfeel lifts the Trumpet to his lips,
Not now to terrify, or to destroy,   210
But raise the dead to judgment, and to Heaven,
Or to Jahennem's purifying flames.

CANTO II.

THE SIRAHT.

Israhfeel stands before the Throne of God,
And through all Heavens and Earths the Trumpet peals,
And angels, men, and Jinn, the Trumpet hear,   215
And every one awakes to conscious life.
Some to the heavens exulting raise their looks:
Some on their faces fall, and call the earth
To gape and swallow them. The good appear
With faces bright as day; the wicked stand   220
With faces blacker than the blasted sun. [80]
   And now the Throne, still veiled in light, descends,
Upborne by all good angels, to the earth:
For on the highest earth is doom pronounced,
Alike upon the children of the earth,   225
And those of light and fire. The Throne is set,
And now an awful Voice is heard by all:
"Let the six lower earths at once give up
The angels and the Jinn that they contain!"
   Now Iblees and his troops in terror rise,   230
And take their place upon the highest earth.
   Again proclaimed the solemn Voice of God,
Heard clear and loud by all the assembled worlds:
"Sarsar, avenging Wind, thy work is done!
Thou, with the Second and the Seventh Earths,   235
No more art needed!" These were swept away.
The Voice continued, "Sulphur, Serpents, Stones,
And Scorpions, seek Jahennem! Adam's race!
Behold the narrow bridge Siraht, that lies
From Earth to Heaven, above the pit of Hell!   240

The Bridge itself shall judge you as you pass.
Alone, O Eesa, stay! Thou needest not
To cross the awful Bridge. Approach this Throne,
And view all other reasoning beings pass!"
And Eesa went and stood before the Throne.   245
   Across Jahennem lay the awful Bridge,
From Kahf to Heaven, and under the Siraht,
The quenchless fires were flaming, and a stench
Appalling issued from the depths of Hell.
The Bridge was finer than a spider's web,   250
Long as from Kahf to Kahf, and all begirt
With thorns and briars, and sharper than a sword.
   First passed the human race. With lightning speed,
Some darted fearlessly across the Bridge;
While others, yielding to a force unseen   255
That forced them on the Bridge against their will,
Wearied at length, and torn by thorns and briars,
Down to their destined dungeons headlong fell;
While at each fall, the flaming gulf below
Cast sparks as large as camels round the Bridge.   260
   The human race had all passed o'er the gulf,
When spoke again the solemn Voice of God.
"Angels of God, advance upon the Bridge!
Angels and Jinn, your wings are useless here,
And all who dare to fly across the gulf,   265
Shall surely fall!"
            They heard the dread command,
And crossed. In safety all passed o'er, but those
Who fell with Iblees. These the abyss engulphed,
And buried in the lowest Hell of all.
Among the angels who in safety walked,   270
Hahroot and Mahroot [58] passed among the rest;

And Iblees, when he saw that both were safe,
O'ercome with rage and fury gnashed his teeth,
In fruitless envy and despair. Again
The Voice was heard from God's eternal Throne. 275
  "Pass the Siraht, O ye Believing Jinn,
Led by the King to whom you owe your faith!"
  Then Ed-Dimiryaht instantly passed o'er,
With all his troops, nor feared that awful Bridge;
And none of all his numerous followers sank   280
Amid the seething, flaming stones below.
  Once more they heard the awful Voice proclaim,
"If any true believer 'mid the troops
Of Iblees stands, let him before the rest,
Unfearing tread the awful Bridge of Breadth!"   285
Zelemboor, Balkees, Dahish heard the call,
And many more of lesser note than these,
Passed safely o'er the gulf of raging flame.
  Iblees and all his troops in wild despair,
With envious glances filled with hate and rage,   290
Beheld themselves the last to cross the Bridge:
But envy and despair oppressed them worst,
When angels or when Jinn who once had sinned,
In safety trod the Bridge they feared to tread.
  Dahish, who fell not from the Bridge, sprang up, 295
And joyfully to Ed-Dimiryaht flew.
"I owe to thee repentance and my faith,
O mighty King of the Believing Jinn!
Thou gavest me my punishment on earth,
And therefore I escape the flames of Hell."   300
  "O Dahish, thank not me," the King replied.
"Thy thanks are due to God alone. To Him
Give all the glory! I did but fulfil

His Prophet's wise commandment. Thank not me,
But unto God alone be all the praise!"   305
Then Dahish answered, "Thou art in the right:
But thou the fated instrument hast been
Of my repentance; and for this I give
My thanks to thee, although full well I know
That God foredoomed my earthly destiny.   310
And now I stand before thee here. I passed
The Bridge, and by my punishment on earth,
Like Hahroot and like Mahroot I am saved!"
He spoke, and Ed-Dimiryaht turned away,
And gazed upon the Bridge with anxious look,   315
As Iblees and the Evil Jinn advanced
On the Siraht with most unwilling steps.
But Iblees would not even now obey
The strict command to walk across the Bridge.
Resolved to be a rebel to the last,   320
He strove to fly across the fiery gulf.
The air was all too thin to bear his weight,
And wearied to the utmost, down he sank
Before his troops. But soon as all had placed
On the Siraht their feet, it sways and heaves   325
Beneath their tread, then snaps at either end,
And in the fathomless abyss it falls,
And o'er it rush the waves of flaming stone,
And a thick cloud of darkness veils the gulf.
The lower earths have all been whelmed in Hell: 330
The highest earth alone remains behind:
A ray shines on it from the Throne of God,
And it becomes a Heaven. The Throne is raised
Again above the Heavens. Then Azraeel takes
The golden Key to which his Sword had changed, 335

And wide he throws the gate of Heaven itself,
For those who passed the gulf.
              Distinctions now,
Are swept away, and angels, men, and Jinn,
Form but a single race. But o'er their joy
A shade is cast, for still they think of those   340
Who drink the boiling water, and devour
The Zakkoom fruit accursed. Iblees still,
And those around him in the lowest Hell,
Against all hope, still hope to reascend,
And cast the Throne of Allah into Hell,   345
And consummate their wickedness, not yet
Subdued by torments; though most anxiously
Do all in Heaven await the destined time
When Heaven shall open to receive the lost,
Raised from Jahennem, never more to sin.   350
    Joharahbahd might not compare with Heaven,
And all the joys of earth and Jinneestahn,
Would seem as nought beside it. Yet 'tis said,
That when Jahennem shall be swept away,
Then shall the joys of all eternity,   355
Unfold before the blessed universe,
Now pure from sin and woe for evermore.
Then too, the veil of light that wraps the Throne,
Shall pass away, and thus to sight unfold,
In all its glory, not to be endured,   360
Its inconceivable magnificence,
That not the blessed have the strength to bear,
Until Jahennem's utterly destroyed,
When perfect bliss shall dawn on every soul.
    The wicked in Jahennem one by one   365
Work out their own redemption, and the Hells

Are gradually destroyed, and six are gone,
And Iblees and his sons alone remain,
Whelmed in the Seventh Hell, the Hell of Hells,
For demons and for hypocrites reserved.   370

———

CANTO III.

JAHENNEM.

IBLEES and all his sons are sunk in Hell:
(Zelemboor only safely trod the Bridge:)
No resolution can the torment bear
A moment, and the everlasting pain
Can nothing temper; but within themselves,   375
Their sufferings are far greater from despair,
And that remorse which only comes too late,
And rage and hatred and unconquered pride,
Than from the stone-fed flames in which they lie,
Whelmed in the deepest gulf of all in Hell.   380
Above them spreads the flaming Zakkoom tree,
Its fruits the heads of serpents; and from these,
A burning venom drips, an endless spring
Of liquid poison, that corrodes and eats
Like strongest acid, wheresoe'er it falls.   385
And every one attempts to avoid the juice,
And each to shun the flames that roar around.
Their chains are clashing, and the fearful sounds
Of chains, and cries, and roaring flames are heard
Unceasing, while the snakes and scorpions coil   390
Round Iblees and his sons; and brimstone fires

Light up the abhorrent scene a ghastly blue.
　　Dahsim was first among them to perceive
That it was all in vain to strive against
The abyss of flame. The boiling water springs　　395
Let fall a cataract of seething foam,
O'er Iblees and his sons; and all must drink,
(As thirsty camels drink,) the boiling flood.
The boiling liquid makes their tortures worse,
And heated to the utmost pitch, it rends　　400
Its way through every tissue, and is free
To form an overwhelming cataract,
Again to enter on its course of wrath.
　　Dahsim at length perceives that all his woe
Has been deserved, and knows resistance vain,　　405
Yet thinking those around him suffer more,
He throws himself before the boiling flood,
That all its torture may be poured on him.
And warded from his brethren for a time.
Then by his brother's generous action moved,　　410
El Aawar strives to aid him; but the flood
Avoids them both. Their shoes of glowing steel,
(Those shoes which made their sculls like caldrons boil),
Fall from their feet. The floor beneath them heaves,
And far from their companions are they hurled.　　415
　　Then cried El Aawar, "Dahsim, I perceive
That Allah still beholds us even here,
Or wherefore should he mitigate our pain?
There may he hope for pardon still for us,
And those who yet endure the fearful pains,　　420
Of which we surely have escaped the worst.
O God, my pride is utterly destroyed!
O give me back the innocence I lost,

And I will rest contented in the flames
That rage around me! Sin is worse than pain.   425
Did I not feel the might of Purity,
When under a Jinneeyeh's arm I fell?
Did not Meymooneh face the Seal itself,
And drive e'en Faktash back before her flames?
O grant me, God, the purity of Heaven,   430
Or take my life away! 1 cannot bear
To live in sin! My brother, let us pray,
And He who sits above the Seventh Heaven,
Will surely hear, and pity those who kneel
Before him, all submissive to his power!"   435
 Bound in their chains of burning adamant,
They knelt amid the flaming stones of Hell;
And God, who ne'er o'erlooks a sinner's cry,
Called Ed-Dimiryaht up before his Throne.
 "Jinnee, thy ceaseless prayers for those who lie   440
Amid Jahennem's raging flames, are heard.
Look down, and side by side shall thou behold
El Aawar, and his brother Dahsim kneel.
'Tis thine to lead them from Jahennem's flames;
Nor fear to do so, for the flames torment   445
The wicked in proportion to their guilt,
And virtuous souls might lie for endless years,
Unhurt amid the greatest pains in Hell."
 The Jinnee looked, and every Heaven became
As clear as glass, and as he looked, he saw   450
El Aawar kneel by Dahsim.
                              "Praise to thee,
Who hearest e'en the prayers of those in Hell,
And for a heart of stone canst give them flesh!
Unbounded are thy mercies, and their sum

Is never to be numbered, O my God!"   455
Then from the light that still concealed the Throne,
He turned, and with his utmost speed he flew
Down to Jahennem, and appeared before
The sons of Iblees, while the flames of Hell
Leaped harmlessly around him.
                                   "I have come,   460
Commissioned from the Holy One," he cried,
"To free you from this fearful pit of woe;
And Heaven's exulting gates will widely ope
To admit repentant sinners. Greater joy,
Than welcoming repentant sinners home,   465
We know not yet. Israhfeel will announce
To all, this mighty triumph over Hell,
With his melodious, soul-entrancing songs."
   As Ed-Dimiryaht spoke, their burning chains,
Half melted as they were with fervent heat,   470
From off the limbs of both in fragments fell.
"Now," Ed-Dimiryaht cried "your wings are free!
Come, follow me to Heaven, and endless peace.
Soon will your father and your brethren join
The blest above; and then shall perfect bliss   475
For ever reign, when Heaven expands its bounds
Throughout the universe."
                                   And as he spoke,
His wings he spread, and from the gulf he rose,
And led the way to Heaven; and as he flew,
Behind him Dahsim and El Aawar came,   480
Forgetting in their joy the flames of Hell,
But mourning still for Iblees, Teer, and Soht.
   Marjahneh sat with Balkees, and they spoke
Of earth, and all their past, and then agreed

To rise before the Throne and pray for those   485
Who lay amid the flames; but as they talked,
Came Eesa to them, and they bowed before
The holiest of mankind. A lofty peace,
And love and joy that nought could ever change,
Were plain to all who looked upon his face: 490
And when he spoke, 'twas plain to all who heard,
His inmost thoughts were in his words expressed.
　"Know, O Jinneeyehs, God has heard your prayers,
For Ed-Dimiryaht, even as I speak,
Is leading Dahsim and El Aawar up   495
To where you stand."
　　　　　　And Balkees then exclaimed,
"When shall I see my father Iblees here,
And all the sin that causes Hell, destroyed,
O best and noblest of the race of men?"
　He answered, "Yet a little must thou wait;   500
For Teer and Soht must first be raised to Heaven,
And Iblees last; but then shall Hell itself,
Be swept away, and ne'er be raised again.
O Father, thou art Everlasting Love,
And e'en Jahennem's vaults thy mercy built,   505
To purify from every taint of sin,
Those who when saved shall bless thee evermore!"
　As Eesa spoke, the rush of wings was heard,
And speechless with excess of love and joy,
Marjahneh sprang into her father's arms,   510
And she was Dahsim's daughter once again,
Nor would she ever need to dread him more.
Marjahneh could not speak, but soaring up,
She led her father to the eternal Throne;
Then followed all their friends, and Eesa's face   515

Beamed yet a lovelier lustre at the sight.

Soht was the next of Iblees' sons who felt
How greatly he deserved the pains of Hell;
Aud thinking his companions must endure
Far greater pains than he, he sought to shield   520
His father Iblees from the poison-dew,
Fast dropping from the accursed Zakkoom tree.
The heart of Teer was softened at the sight,
And he essayed to stem the boiling flood,
And ward it from his father, who endured   525
The fiercest tortures of the lowest Hell.
Again the floor heaved up, and Iblees lay
Alone within his dungeon, for his sons
Were cast far distant from him. They perceived
Their shoes were gone, the Zakkoom touched them not, 530
And half their pain remitted. Where they stood,
They sang a hymn of thankfulness and praise
To God; and as they sang, their breaking chains,
Fell at their feet, and far away they saw
The light of Heaven above them. Up they sprang, 535
And when they reached the ray of holy light,
They found themselves in Heaven, and wholly freed
From all Jahennem's agonising pains.

But Iblees in his fiery dungeon lay,
The boiling water melting every nerve,   540
In inconceivable despair, to which
The boiling water could not be compared
For torture, nor the shoes of glowing steel,
Which made his scull as 'twere a caldron boil;
Nor yet the Zakkoom's pestilential juice,   545
Nor e'en the sulphur not to be consumed,
In which he lay, nor yet the burning stones,

Nor could the infernal snakes and scorpions cause
Such agony as his despair. At length
He thought of all the good he might have wrought, 550
And how his powers had all been turned to sin,
And he rebelled against his rightful Lord,
And in his mad rebellion, dragged his sons,
And all who listened to his evil words,
To sin and woe. He knew that he deserved   555
Worse pains than he endured; but now he feared,
The innocence and virtue he had lost,
Could never more be his. When this he felt,
He madly strove to conquer the despair
That filled him at the thought; but all in vain   560
He threw himself amid the thickest flames,
For outward torments cannot touch despair!
At length he felt himself subdued, and wept, —
Wept for the virtue he so long had lost,
And for unnumbered sins. But instantly   565
The load lay lighter on him, and the snakes
And scorpions fled; his chains and shoes fell off;
The sulphur inconsumable dissolved
Before the tears; the cursed Zakkoom juice,
Fell on him now no longer, and the flood   570
Of boiling water stopped its fearful course.
The stones grow cold, the raging flames are quenched,
And Iblees stands no more in pain, but freed
Alike from pain and sin: yet still he weeps,
And for redemption and forgiveness prays.   575
That prayer was heard; Jahennem passed away;
And Heaven remains and fills the universe;
And Iblees stands delivered from his sins;
Iblees no longer, but El Hahrith called,

As when he sinless was in former time,   580
Ere yet his pride had hurled him from above,
Despairingly to range the earth, and drag
Jinn, angels, men with him to Hell below.
    Then, 'mid the exulting songs of all in Heaven,
Did Balkees welcome him to endless joy!   585

CANTO IV.

THE CONSUMMATION.

TIME is no more, and Love has conquered Hell,
And every evil world is swept away,
And Heaven extends throughout the universe.
No longer matter, time, and space are chains:
Their temporal might is gone for evermore.   590
Nor do the races sprung from light and fire,
And those from earth, as formerly, remain
Apart, for all distinctions are destroyed.
Now is the veil uplifted from the Throne,
And a transparent light beams over all,   595
That nothing can compare with, nor produce,
Except the Throne, an emblem as it is,
Of the great omnipresent primal Soul.
But even Eesa sees no form revealed.
Around the happy this eternal light   600
Is spread, and they with God converse in soul,
For all can feel the Universal Life
That mingles with their souls, and feel with awe,
That God himself is speaking to their hearts.

In close communion, never more to cease.   605
The deadliest foes on earth are greatest friends,
And every heart is open; all can see
The inmost feelings of another's soul,
E'en as on earth we see a human face!
The power to live for self is all unknown,   610
For in promoting joy, but virtue more,
They but promote their own. No talisman
Is needed to control the race of Jinn;
For having passed through Hell's terrific flames,
The wicked all their wickedness have lost.   615
And ever speaks the eternal Mind of God,
To all in Heaven: "Continue in the way
Of righteousness and progress evermore!
All obstacles are gone, and ye are now
The sons of God for ever. Nought can touch   620
Your spotless virtue. That itself ye feel,
Reward enough for all the cares of earth."
    Those who on earth have felt the eternal Mind,
The most, are greatest now, and strive to raise
Those who are yet below them in the scale   625
Of joy and virtue, higher than the point
That they themselves have reached. For ever on!
Development and progress never cease,
In Heaven or Earth; and this eternal law,
The mainspring of this glorious universe,   630
Unchanged shall last throughout eternity.
    To God in his infinity, rolls on
The endless progress of immortal souls:
And infinite as God himself its course,
For to his greatness it may ne'er approach,   635
The Archangels still grow nobler than before:

12

The angels, and the sons of earth and fire,
Alike. The dread solemnity has left
The face of Azraeel, and no more 'tis said,
That he of all the angels ne'er can smile: 64(
For all acknowledge that his golden Key,
Though formed from his resistless Sword of flame,
For them unbarred the eternal gates of Heaven.
The former Heaven was all unlike to this,
To which e'en angels had to pass through death,   645
And cross the dread Siraht, the Bridge of Breadth.
    Nearest to God himself works Eesa still,
And subject but to Him alone, he rules,
The race of Adam, now no longer weak;
And Ed-Dimiryaht rules the race of Jinn;   650
The Archangels rule the angels; but they rule
As best and noblest of the assembled worlds,
Which thus they govern, not by fear but love.
    But e'en the Archangels yield to Eesa's power;
The power of goodness: yet not he is King,   655
But God alone, who speaks to every heart,
And trains it to obedience to his will.
Yet is this not subservience; love alone
Directs the universe from which is cleansed
Whate'er had power to clog its endless course: 660
For mutual love and virtue are the joys
That Heaven presents to all. On these alone,
The order of the universe depends,
E'en now; and when all sin and woe are gone,
How mightily shall love and virtue rule!   665
    What are the afflictions of a life on earth?
E'en as the faded blossoms of a tree,
Which must be scattered, ere the immortal fruit

Can spring to all luxuriance in the sun
Of God's eternal goodness, and the love   670
Which he bestows on all in Earth and Heaven,
And all in all the worlds that he has sown
Through endless space, beyond our twilight sphere.
  And while God's children work thus gloriously,
Shall Eesa and his Father gaze on all,   675
In love and joy and glory none can speak.
Eternally the work of all shall last,
Eternal as their innocence and joy,
Which must endure, while with unbounded love,
Shall God and Eesa watch the assembled worlds,   680
And approbation upon all things smile.
And God shall see his creatures in their joy,
And as his voice shall speak them "very good!"
Shall Eesa, with a heart that overflows
With love to all, reflect the immortal smile   685
Of God upon the eternal universe,
Brightening for ever in his changeless love!

END OF THE SIXTH BOOK.

NOTES TO ED-DIMIRYAHT.

THE information contained in the following Notes, when not acknowledged, is taken either from the Arabian Nights, and Lane's
or Trébutien's notes (especially Lane's notes 2 and 21 to, the Intro-
duction); or from the Kuran, and Lane's or Sale's notes, and the
Preliminary Discourse of the latter.

1. Jann Ibn Jann was the last of forty, or according to other
accounts, seventy-two preadamite kings of the Jinn (comp. note 4.)
In the poem, I have called him, for euphony, Jarjarees, which is
the name of an Efreet in the Arabian Nights. This king rebelled
against God, and was defeated and slain in battle by the angels.
In this battle Azazeel, or El Harith (afterwards Iblees, vide note
3) was taken prisoner; and I think some say he was a son of Jann
Ibn Jann. But the accounts of Iblees differ very much.

2. In the Mohammadan cosmogony there are seven heavens,
earths, and hells. This earth is the highest of the earths; the second contains the freezing wind called the Sarsar (vide Southey's
Thalaba, book 1.), the third, the stones which are to form the fuel
of Jahennem (or hell); the fourth, its sulphur; the fifth, its serpents;
the sixth its scorpions; and the seventh, Iblees and his followers.
The accounts of hell differ; but all agree that the seventh is for
hypocrites. Over the Seventh Heaven spreads the Empyrean of
the Throne of God.

3. When the angels defeated Jann Ibn Jann, (vide note 1), they
brought Azazeel to Heaven, where he attained a very high dignity.
He refused at length to do homage to Adam, whereupon God
cursed and banished him, changing his name to Iblees (Despair.)
All who abetted him fell with him.

4. There are supposed to be three classes of reasoning beings;
angels created of light, Jinn of fire, and men of earth. Men form
the highest class. All classes are more or less mortal. The terms
here employed for Jinn are Jinnee and Jinneeyeh, the masculine

and feminine appellations respectively; and Efreet, a term used generally, but not exclusively, for a powerful evil Jinnee.

5. Fire circulates in the veins of the Jinn instead of blood. With this they fight, and when a Jinnee receives a mortal wound; his own fire bursts from it, and burns him to ashes. They are said to be created of s m o k e l e s s fire (that of the Samoom); but smoke is mentioned in all accounts of their battles.

6. The Zakkoom is a tree growing out of the midst of hell. Its leaves and branches are of flaming fire, and its fruit resembles the heads of serpents.

7. Iblees has five sons; Teer, who causes calamities, losses and injuries; El Aawar, who encourages debauchery; Sot, who superintends lying; Dasim, who causes hatred between man and wife; and Zelemboor, who presides over places of traffic. Besides these, several others ore mentioned in Oriental tales.

8. A species of tree which abounds in heaven, according to the Kuran.

9. Ed-Dimiryat is mentioned in the Arabian Nights (Story of the City of Brass), as the king of the Jinn, and the wezeer (or vizior) of Suleyman (vide note 20). His daughter Meymooneh, (Story of Kamar Ez-Zeman) is called an Efreeteh, and a descendant of Iblees. Milton's Abdiel did not suggest this character; but I have purposely endeavoured to make the two as unlike as the exigencies of the poem would permit.

10. Marjaneh is a very common name in Eastern tales, and has several meanings. As one of these is "a small pearl", the word is perhaps connected with the Latin Margarita?

11. There are four Archangels, Jebraeel, the angel of Revelations; Meekaeel, the patron of the Israelites; Azraeel, the angel of death, and Israfeel, the angel of the Trumpet.

According to Jewish traditions, the sword of the angel of death has three drops of gall at the end, which fall into the mouth of a dying man; one kills him, another turns him pale, and the third putrefies him. (Southey's Thalaba, I. 52, and note.)

12. The Jinn, good and bad alike, had unrestricted admission into heaven till the birth of Christ, when they were excluded from the three highest: and at the birth of Mohammad, they were forbidden the remainder.

13. The forbidden fruit is said by some Mohammadans to have been the vine.

14. "Now go thy way, Abdaldar,

    Servant of Eblis!

    Over Arabia,

    Seek the Destroyer!"   Thalaba, II. 28.

15. Adam and Eve were originally placed in heaven.

16 At the day of judgment all will have to cross the Bridge Sirat, from earth to heaven, over hell. It is finer than a hair, as long as earth is broad, (i. e. five hundred year's journey), sharper than a sword, and girt with thorns and briars. I do not remember where I have seen it called "the Bridge of Breadth", but I believe the true meaning of the word Es-Sirat, is simply "the Straight Path."

17. The allusion here is to Schiller's ballad, "The Diver."

18. I need scarcely mention that the Mohammadans are not Universalists.

19. Moses .

20. Suleyman Ibn Daood is King Solomon. He had a seal-ring inscribed with the mystical name of God, which gave him power to rule over all living creatures and to understand their language.

21. A table in the Seventh Heaven, on which everything is wrtten in letters of light, in a mysterious language. (Southey's Thalaba, X. 24, and note).

22. Jesus Christ.

23. Israfecl has a heart of lute-strings, and the sweetest voice of any of God's creatures. At the end of the world he will sound the trumpet three times. The first blast, the Blast of Consternation, (vide book VI., canto I.), will convulse all nature ; the second, the Blast of Annihilation, will kill every living thing; and the third, the Blast of Resurrection, forty years later, will raise the dead. According to other accounts, the trumpet will only be sounded twice. -

24. For a description of Mount Kaf, see book I. canto 4, and book V, canto 2. "From Kaf to Kaf" is a common periphrasis for the whole earth. Kaf is also used as a name for the Caucasus; and European Orientalists frequently confound this with it.

25. It was the buckler of Jann Ibn Jann that the Persian king Tahumers or Tahmuras took with him to Jinnistan, when he went o fight the Deevs. (D'Herbelot and Richardson).

26. The angels drive away the evil Jinn, when they approach the lowest heaven to listen to their conversation, with shooting stars.

"But God gave permission to some angels to cast at the Efreet a shooting star of fire, and he was burnt." Arab. Nights.

> "Fleeter than the starry brands,
> Flung at night from angel hands
> At those dark and daring sprites
> Who would climb the empyreal heights."
> Lalla Rookh.

27. Jinnistan is properly a Persian fairy-land. (D'Herbelot and Richardson; Lalla Rookh, notes 195, 327). Moore's Peristan is, I suspect, a coined word.

28. Story of Es-Sindibad, in the Arabian Nights.

29. "Simorg Anka, says Mr. Fox in a note to Achmed Ardebeili, is a bird or griffin of extraordinary strength and size (as its name imports, signifying as large as thirty eagles), which according to the Eastern writers, was sent by the Supreme Being to subdue and chastise the rebellious Dives. It was supposed to possess rational faculties, and the gift of speech. The Caherman Namch relates that Simorg Anka being asked his [her] age, replied, this world is very ancient, for it has already been seven times replenished with beings different from men, and as often depopulated. That the age of Adam in which we now are is to endure 7000 years, making a great cycle; that he himself [she] had seen twelve of these revolutions, and knew not how many more he [she] had to see." Southey, after quoting the above passage in a note on Thalaba, XI. 12, with his own comments, gives his reasons for considering the Seemurgh distinct from the Rukh; and with all due deference to Mr. Lane, who considers them identical, I am inclined to agree with Southey on this point.

30.   "The diamond turrets of Shadukiam,
>   And the fragant bowers of Amberabad."
> Lalla Rookh.

Vide also Lalla Rookh, notes 195 and 327.

I have no authority for making Amberabad a submarine city.

31. "— tearless raimbows such as span
>   The unclouded skies of Peristan." Lalla Rookh.

"Where the rain never fell, and the wind never blew."
                    Hogg's Queen's Wake: Kilmeny.

32. Saleh is mentioned as a powerful king of the Diving Jinn, in the story of Jullanar (or Gulnare) in the Arabian Nights.

33. In the western parts of the earth is a district called the Regions of Darkness, in which the Throne of Ihlees in placed. The western part of the Circumambient Ocean is called the Sea of Darkness.

34. Meymooneh is a name corresponding to Fortunata in Latin.

35. A common way of summoning Jinn is to throw a little of their hair, or some incense received from them, on a fire. Perhaps this is a notion derived from the times of Arab Paganism?

36. The Jinn can pass through solid substances.

37. The foes of England have more than once acknowledged after a defeat, "If the English knew when they were beaten, we should never have lost the battle."

38. Thora is a common name in the north of Europe to the present day.

39.   "Fain would I fly from mortal sight
          To my own sweet bowers of Peristan,
          But there the flowers are all too bright
          For the eyes of a baby born of man.
          On flowers of earth her feet must tread."
                    Lalla Rookh, preface.

40. "Some sparks struck us both from her and from him: her sparks did us no harm." Arab. Nights.

41. The naked eye can no more bear the light of a lime-ball, than that of the sun; but when held between the eye und the sun and viewed trough a darkened glass, a lime-ball looks like a black spot on the sun. (Lardner's Chemistry.)

42.   "She waked on a couch of the silk sae slim,
          All striped wi' the bars of the rainbow's rim."
                    Hogg's Kilmeny.

43.   "And now my love, my seraph-fair, arise."
                    Keats' Eve of St. Agnes.

44. Asaf, the son of Barkhiya, is constantly mentioned in Oriental tales as the wezeer of Suleyman.

45. This story, as well as some others concerning the building of the Temple, &c., may be found in the Kuran, ch. 34 and 38; and notes.

46. Similar magical articles are common in the fairy tales of all nations.

47. The evil Jinn used always to destroy at night whatever they did in the daytime, if not prevented. When they rebelled against Suleyman, imprisoning in a bottle was the usual punishment.

In line 181, I discovered, when too late to correct it, that I had inadvertently spoken of the Dead Sea as lying south-west, instead of south-east of Jerusalem.

48. This canto is mainly a paraphrase of the episode of Dahish, in the Story of the City of Brass, in the Arabian Nights. This is the nucleus of the whole poem, as Ed-Dimiryat is not mentioned in any other tale I have met with, except simply as Meymooneh's father in that of Kamar Ez-Zeman.

49. Servant of El Harith. The king is not named in the original.

50. A bargain for a wife invariably forms part of a treaty attributed to Solomon in any Eastern tale.

51. In the original, Ed-Dimiryat pursues Dahish for three months before he overtakes him.

52. The story on which the five following cantos are founded, may be found in Sale's Koran, ch. 38, and note. I have changed the name of the Jinnee from Sakhr to Faktash, for enphony. Faktash, like Jarjarees, is the name of an Efreet mentioned in the Arabian Nights.

53. This very singular story is from Sale's Koran, ch. 31, note.

54. Thunder is or was said by some philosophers to be caused by the air closing behind a flash of lightning.

55. "Their breath came thick and fast and their nails turned purple. The blue sky had vanished, that is, the blue sky as we see it, and a blue, deeper than lapis lazuli lay all around them." Extract from a paper in "All the Year Round," descriptive of a balloon ascent.

56. Rings enabling men to live in the sea are mentioned in the story of Jullanar.

57. I have read a story somewhere of a trial of skill between

Richard I. and Salah Ed-Deen, or Saladin. Richard clove an anvil at a blow; and Saladin threw a silk veil into the air, and divided it with his scymitar as it fell.

58· The angels being indignant at human wickedness, God sent two named Haroot and Maroot to judge among men; but on being tempted by the planet Venus in a human form, they fell, and obtained permission from God, to choose their punishment in this world or the next. They are consequently doing penance till the day of judgment.

59. There are several descriptions of submarine cities in the Arabian Nights. Southey has one, also in the Curse of Kehama, book 16. Any allusions to natural objects are here simply taken from British marine natural history.

60. As we advance further between or beyond the tide-marks, we find the marine fauna and flora mapped out in districts, according to the depth, or the length of time they are under water.

61. P h y l l o d o c e, A p h r o d i t e, S e r p u l a and other genera of Annelida.

62. In the original, it is the Lake of Tiberias. It is necessary here to mention that the concluding portion of this canto was written in the spring of 1863, and has not been altered since.

63. The groundwork of this story is given pretty fully in Sale's Koran, ch. 27, and notes.

64· This is only another form of the name Balkees, which occurs in book 5; but I thought it better to keep them distinct.

65. The mention of g l a s s at this period, is I believe, an anachronism; but I am not answerable for it. Weil, in his Biblische Legenden says the floor was of crystal.

66. According to Sale, this Efreet was Sakhr. If so, this canto belongs to an earlier period in the mythical history of Solomon than I have assigned to it. Weil also places it earlier than his marriage with Jerada.

67. This romantic use of the hair is frequent in Oriental tales. See, for instance, the meeting of Zal and Rudabeh, in Firdausee's Shah Nameh. (Atkinson's translation, p. 84.)

> "She flung him down her long black hair,
>   Exclaiming breathless, 'There, love, there!'"
>   Lalla Rookh.

68. I have considerahly lengthened the traditional reign of Solomon, for obvious reasons.

69. This story is from Sales's Koran, ch. 34, and notes.

70. A supernatural animal, whose appearance will be one sign of the approaching end of the world.

71. See the Story of Bulookiya, in Arab. Nights.

72. The story here versified is taken from a note to Southey's Joan of Arc, book VI.

Iskender is Alexander the Great; but he is often confounded with a mythical hero of the time of Abraham; and the same exploits are attributed indiscriminately to both. I have here substituted Caucasus for Kaf, the uame used for the mountain alluded to in the original, as more consistant with the wholly human nature of Alexander in this legend. The Fountain of Youth is said to be situated in the Regions of Darkness (vide note 33).

73. The accounts of Ilyas, and El Khidr, or El Khadir, as he is otherwise called, differ very much. I have followed the story cited in the last note.

74. In the Story of Hasan of El Basrah, in the Arabian Nights, Balkees is mentioned as a daughter of Iblees, who married a descendant of Asaf. Hasan of Damascus, and Abd-Allah are both imaginary characters.

75. See the Stories of Seyf El Mulook, and Janshah, in the Arabian Nights. The Queen of Sheba, according to a story in Weber's Eastern Tales was descended from a Jinneeyeh, or a Peree. Weil says her mother was a Jinneeyeh.

76. "Now I am standing on the shore of an ocean of still fire. The stillness that hangs over it seems never to have been broken.

"It does move, however. It ebbs and flows like the ocean. . . . . . . There is a space, strange to say, between this ocean and the superincumbent mass, and in its heavings to and fro it is depositing rock all the time.

"It is not always calm: there are storms at times, when it surges and dashes with great fury." Denton's Nature's Secrets, pp, 267—269.

77. Mountains and seas of metal are spoken of in the Adventures of Hatim Tai, book V.

78. Iskender, (not Alexander the Great; but vide note 72,) constructed a barrier against, the nations of Gog and Magog; but they will break through it at the end of the world, and overrun the

earth with their armies. Trees with sword-leaves, and others bearing fruit in the shape of human beings, are often mentioned in
Oriental works.

79. See the Story of Es-Sindibad, that of Seyf El Mulook, and
other travellers' tales in the Arabian Nights; and Lane's notes
thereupon.

80. The Mohammadan belief that the wicked will appear with
black faces on the day of judgment, explains the meaning of the
common Eastern imprecation, "May God blacken thy face!"

ALCYONE.

PART I. THE FRIENDS.

As free as a land on earth may be,
Is that of the rulers of the sea:
No foe may dare to invade its strand,
And hope to regain his native land;
And well may the tyrant crouch in fear,
When the voice of that nation has reached his ear,
For the proudest have refuge sought in flight,
Who dared to oppose the Sea-Queen's might:
And let the oppressors of men beware,
When rises the Lion in wrath from his lair!   10
    An army has sailed from that western land,
To wrest the sword from a tyrant's hand;
And one day's work has been nobly done,
And yet the contest is scarce begun.
The night has come, and the parted foes
Have gone to their tents to seek repose;
And save for the sentinel's heavy tread,
The camp is still as though all were dead.
The moon looked down in a silver flood,
    On the army that filled the plain;   20
But all that army shall wade in blood,
    Before she shall rise again!

Two youths have quitted their homes, to fight;
To conquer or die, but hold the right.
The younger humble and trusting, mild,
And scarcely in years beyond a child,
Looked up to his friend with a childlike love.
The thoughts of that friend were fixed above.
His soul would from earth soar far away,
Where suns are burning in endless day.   30
Together the friends had dwelt for years,
And shared in common their hopes and fears.
The younger, wearied and spent with fight,
Was sleeping away the silent night.
He lay in his tent, but beside his bed,
His unsheathed sword-blade is reeking red!
But Michael stood by the open door,
And viewed the camp he should see no more.
He showed not a trace of earthly fear,
Though foes unnumbered were sleeping near.   40
His eyes had a proud, yet dreamy look,
And he held in his hand an open book.
Twas Homer, — but all unheeded now:
He raised to the heavens his lofty brow,
And gazing afar in the distant sky,
The group of the Pleiades caught his eye;
And proudly viewing the stars above,
He sang a lay to no earthly love.
"I come from a distant, dear-loved land,
    To fight on a foreign plain,   50
And lead to the charge a gallant band,
    I never may lead again.
O star above me shining,
    Beyond thy fellows bright;

Ten myriad orbs thou leadest,
Curbed by thy chains of light.
Perchance the eve of another day
I never again may see;
But if I should fall in the bloody fray,
O star, I will fly to thee!   60
But thou, although a Central Sun,
Obey'st a mightier will:
The work of God which thou hast done,
'Tis thine to still fulfil.
Alcyone, surrounded
By worlds of glowing light!
I love thee more than any star
That ever lit the night."
Then Arthur from his sleep awoke,
And thus to Michael anxious spoke: 70
"Shall men be free when they burst a chain
That binds them down to a world of pain?
Shall men be free when they rise on high,
To join in the music of the sky?"
"O doubt not this, for who would care
To live for aye on earth?
Our longing for eternity,
Proclaims a heavenly birth.
The Throne of the universal King
Is fixed in the Central Sun: 80
And those who attain to that world of God,
A glory indeed have won.
But Arthur, although I know not fear,
To-morrow I stand not gazing here:
I feel that the stars are calling away
My spirit to traverse their realms for aye.

No longer is earth my home, but there,
Where worlds unnumbered are beaming fair!"
  "Nay, Michael!" exclaimed the shuddering boy;
"I would not withhold you from such a joy: 90
But, should you perish, if I am dear,
I pray you leave me not lonely here:
But let us by all that's sacred, vow
That nought existing shall part us now!"
By Earth and Heaven, and all therein,
  Did Michael and Arthur swear
That Life, nor Death, nor Eternity,
  To part them should ever dare.
They swore by the Light and Darkness;
  They swore by the Lord of all;   100
They swore by Alcyone's splendour,
  No parting should e'er befall.
  Then Arthur to his tent withdrew,
And girded on his sword anew,
For brighter regions paled away,
Before the rays of earthly day.
But now the trumpet is pealing loud,
  And foes are advancing with hasty speed;
And swift to their posts the heroes crowd;
  And now the armies have met indeed.   110
The air is filled with the iron hail,
And Death is wielding his awful flail;
The swords are clashing, and bayonets gleam
Like a tossing sea in the morning's beam;
And far and wide are the missiles sent,
On errands of deadly purpose bent.
But Michael and Arthur have firm pressed on,
  (Their troop behind), to the hostile front,

Where, gleaming, a fence of bayonets shone,
And few may maintain the battle's brunt.   120
The phalanx they scarce could hope to break:
One desperate charge could the squadron make,
And Michael beheld, and his sword he drew,
And 'mid the bayonets his charger threw.
Six bayonets and more transfixed his steed,
But long before they again were freed,
He vaulted over his horse's head,
And under his feet two foes lay dead.
And grasping his sword with both his hands,
He leaps where the hostile ensign stands.   130
He fights with an English hero's force,
And none may withstand his desperate course.
And the madness of war makes all things glare
    Through a thick red haze, while the crimson blood
Has tinged with its hue his very soul;
    And 'mid the phalanx alone he stood.
Another of Michael's foes was slain;
But ere he could raise his sword again,
A musket-ball crashed through brain and head:
He sank to the ground among the dead.   140
    When Arthur beheld his friend was slain,
He called to the troops behind again,
And rushed at once 'mid the thickest fray:
What cared he then to survive that day?
And over his friend he sternly strode:
The tide of battle against him flowed;
Three foes had fallen beneath his hand,
His troops were making a gallant stand,
When deep in the throat he felt a wound,
That stretched him lifeless upon the ground.   150

But though they died, they had cleared a way
By which their friends could conclude the fray;
For the army behind pressed nobly on,
Their enemies found their advantage gone,
And, breaking their ranks, tumultuous fled:
But half their number abandoned, — dead!

PART II. **THE SUN.**

THE darkness of death has passed away,
And Michael and Arthur awake in day.
They lie not now on the battle-plain,
All red with blood of the foes they've slain;
But flaming round them a glory beams
With lustre beyond all earthly dreams;
Their froms are thinner than purest air,
And wishes convey them everywhere:
To the innermost wreathes of the vaporous sun,
Or the furthest of worlds that around it may run.   10
    And Michael exclaimed, "I am free! I am free!
Alcyone burns in its glory for me!
O dearest of friends, we have broken our chains,
And no longer the burden of matter restrains.
Let us visit these founts of unquenchable light,
And see how the sun is so wondrously bright:
Then view the half-suns that around it must roll,
Till each, like the sun, grows instinct with a soul;
And, lighting the sun-studded caverns of space,
A path through a fathomless ocean shall trace;   20
And each form a Centre to many an earth,
As bright as the world that received us at birth.
Then, quitting the system whose centre is here,
Alcyone seek we, the innermost sphere;
Where the Lord of all nature sits firm on his Throne,
And views the bright worlds that encircle his own.
The lime-light is darkness when held to the sun:
So Sirius pales in the light of the One!"
    Arthur answered, "Wherever you lead me, I go!"
And Michael immediately darted below,   30

13*

Where, sinking amid the vast oceans of flame,
At length to the deepest abysses they came,
Where the Soul of the Sun guides its system for aye,
And fosters the planets wherever they stray,
And guides them when first they emerge from the sun,
Till his mystical office of nurture is done;
And forth from his system the planet is thrown,
To find, as a sun, a new path of its own.
They saw ten thousand spirits fly
To every quarter of the sky;   40
And bear their monarch's mandates far
To every distant wandering star
That owns the ruler of the sun,
Until its planet's course is run.
In a hall of a thousand rainbows,
   The Soul of the Sun bears sway:
His throne of a thousand lightnings
   Was changing its hues alway.
Earth's brightest hues were no longer bright:
   The brightest noon were as midnight dim,   50
Compared with the meanest ray of light,
   The palest radiance that flamed round him!
"O King of the Centre of Planets!
   How best is this goal to be won?
We would fly where Alcyone glitters,
   To worship the Innermost Sun."
"And what though o'er suns of one system,
   Alcyone boasts the control?
Think ye that its far-flashing splendours
   Avail to rule over the Whole!   60
And what though that star flamed around you,
   Your journey were scarcely begun:

For know that Alcyone fettered,
   Rolls round a more glorious Sun.
But still is that star the one Splendour
   That governs the whole Milky Way;
And all of that nebula's rulers
   Alcyone only obey:
But the King who rules over the Kosmos,
   No spirit may visibly view: 70
He spreads o'er the whole of his empire,
   Pervading it everywhere through.
But those who would learn from that Monarch,
   Must wait till he speaks to the soul:
His mind, like the blood of a mortal,
   Flows redly and clear through the Whole.
Go then where Alcyone's burning;
   Beside it, its planets are dim:
And ask the bright angel who guards it,
   What spirit is Lord over him?"   80
"O King of the Centre of Planets!
   How long hast thou ruled in the Sun?
Awaits thee a day in the future,
   When all thy grand task shall be done?"
"1 stand where for ages unending,
   My lot by my Maker was cast:
Before me, an infinite Future;
   Behind me, a measureless Past.
The Earth shall grow into a Centre,
   As bright as this Sun where we stand: 90
The Sun, in a future as distant,
   Shall join a more glorious band:
Perchance, where Alcyone's shining,
   My Kingdom a place may attain;

And, vast as the regions it lightens,
  The regions o'er which I may reign."
  They left the bright monarch, and hastened away
To bathe in the sunlight unclouded for aye.
The depths of the sun were revealed to their sight,
And its fountains they viewed of unquenchable light, 100
And saw how from system to system is hurled
The light that's reflected from many a world,
That not a sun may ever fade,
And cast its planets into shade,
For howsoe'er the light is used,
So exquisitely 'tis diffused,
That not a ray is spent in vain,
But shines reflected back again.
But slowly melts the solar orb,
  And while it melts away,   110
Far brighter grow the rays around,
  And wait a grander day.
For, bright as is its dress of light,
Its very core must grow as bright.
The inmost core as yet is dark,
  But all its heavens as fire:
Go, Michael, Arthur, view those heavens,
  Expanding ever higher!
Around the solid sun there burns
  A blazing lightning sea,   120
While 'mid that dazzling ocean sports
  A wondrous company.
Monsters a thousand miles in length,
  Throughout the lightnings dash.
Which as they cleave the topmost floods,
  Still brighter round them flash.

And lo, a mighty mass of stone,
From some far distant planet thrown,
Drops down upon the lightning sea,
Which closes round it instantly;   130
While such the gleams that round it play,
That ninety million miles away,
The sun appears to gazer's sight,
To shine with twenty times its light:
And now the atmosphere around
Is pressed against the solar ground,
And whirlwinds in a moment part
The clouds of light, which backward start,
And leave the solid nucleus bare:
The monsters swift assemble there,   140
And guide the lightnings till they fly,
Again across that wondrous sky.
    All these, and many wonders more,
The youths beheld on that far shore,
Till Michael cried, "Away, away!
Alcyone is brighter aye;
And we must see the worlds that run
Around their central source, the Sun;
Then to Alcyone we fly,
Though brighter worlds than this are nigh,   150
Nor pause again upon our race,
Until we see its monarch's face."
    "I were weary" said Arthur, "O Michael, alone,
If thou, my dear friend, on a journey wert gone;
And though I believe that the Universe Soul
Is even now with us, pervading the Whole;
Yet, whithersoever you lead me, I go
To regions whose distance no numbers may show."

PART III. **THE INFERIOR PLANETS.**

THEN they quitted the sun, and they touched not the sod,
Until in the forests of Vulcan they trod.
From the north to the south spread a mantle of green,
And nothing but forests and marshes were seen.
The ferns shook their plumes in the rays of the sun,
Which shone through the vapours all faded and dun.
Not yet is the planet so perfect
    That animals dwell on its plains;
And its chord in the music of Heaven,
    Is fitful and harsh in its strains.   10
The angel who watches o'er Vulcan,
    Came forward and welcomed the pair:
"You come to a planet imperfect;
    The others beyond are more fair.
This planet is circled with vapour,
    (And Mercury yet is not clear,)
But this shall condense to an ocean,
    And rational creatures appear.
But Nature moves aye in a circle:
    These clouds shall be scattered away,   20
But the planet be flooded with splendour
    At some very far distant day."
Arthur answered the angel, "Do you, King, desire
The day when your planet shall roll amid fire?"
"I wait for the time, nor impatiently wait
The day when among the bright stars mine is great.
These plants that surround us must wither and fall;
For earthquakes and marshes shall swallow them all.
When man in the fulness of time shall appear,
The coal that shall serve him is waiting him here!"   30

Said Arthur, "We roam on an infinite quest,
Pursuing the Rock on which all things must rest:
The Sun of the Universe ever we seek;
And if thou canst rightly direct us, O speak!"
"Alcyone's far in the distance,
  No particle solid remains;
And its chord, in the Harp of the Kosmos,
  Emits the divinest of strains.
The sun is the King of our system,
  But yet round Alcyone flies: 40
Alcyone's self is a planet
  To systems beyond it that rise.
To Mercury hasten. You never shall learn
The Centre round which the whole Kosmos must turn!"
Away from the marshes of Vulcan,
  The daring adventurers fly;
Away to the planet beyond it,
  That glitters afar in the sky.
Its music, though milder than Vulcan's,
  Is broken and harsh to the ear: 50
Not yet is it peopled with mammals;
  Not yet is its atmosphere clear.
Its angel spoke thus to the strangers:
"Whence come ye, O spirits, and why?
Why seek ye a planet imperfect;
  When others far brighter are nigh?"
"We first to every star would roam,
That finds around the sun its home:
Then in Alcyone we seek
The brighter realms of which you speak;   60
And we would gain the Central Sun,
And then the goal we seek were won!"

"No length of time, or power can bear
The highest solar monarchs there:
How then shall ye, O wanderers, gain
What Sirius' king might seek in vain?"
"We ask not Sirius' king to show
The path on which we ought to go;
Alcyone's alone shall tell
Where greater Kings than he may dwell!"   70
   Thus Michael, proud and haughty, spoke:
The king again the silence broke.
"I do not blame that holy zeal,
Which may you never cease to feel!
But, to succeed upon your quest,
Is hopeless. You will never rest
Until the King you seek shall say,
'Beyond my realms you may not stray!'"
   They viewed the country, but they knew
Of plants that grew around them, few: 80
For Vulcan's plants they saw no more,
Nor earth's as yet adorned that shore:
But strange-shaped beasts were all around,
Slow crawling o'er the marshy ground,
And, darting through the half-formed sea,
The fish the scaly monsters flee,
While reptile birds are in the air,
And reptile forms are everywhere,
Of which the crocodiles of earth,
May represent a later birth.   90
   Then through the dim atmosphere Michael arose,
Till all the sun's glory again round him flows,
And he pointed to Venus. They quickened their flight
Towards the new world that unfolds to their sight;

And as they rapidly draw near,
Its chord of music loud they hear:
No longer harsh, but clear and strong;
It sounded loud, it sounded long,
But much was wanting to complete
Its harmony, though wild and sweet.   100
One long monotonous changeless tone,
That wearied them, was heard alone;
And some discordant notes of fear,
That grated harshly on the ear,
They heard, but nought to indicate
A reasoning creature's love or hate.
But seated at its northern pole,
They saw the imperfect planet's Soul.
   "Ye come from a world that's nearest mine,
Which shares a part of the Soul divine.   110
Ye see how savage and wild a race
Of men in an infant world have place;
Ye see them chasing with weapons rude,
The monsters that form their daily food.
These creatures that now before them flee,
In higher worlds ye may never see.
For larger than earthly beasts are they,
Yet these shall become the glacier's prey;
What earth is now shall my planet be,
In distant ages, which I foresee.   120
When countless ages have rolled away,
My world has a mighty part to play:
And therefore I wait, till men begin
To show their reason; to pray; to sin;
And learn that whate'er may stand or fall,
One mighty Ruler is God of all.

You dare to seek him, O strangers twain:
Perchance we never may meet again;
But take my blessing, and go your way,
For He shall guide you, where'er you stray."   130
    "Farewell, His blessing be on thee,
Whate'er He dooms your world to be!"
They answered, nor remained there long,
For still resolved, with purpose strong,
Rose Michael through the air that holds
The planet Venus in its folds,
And swiftly takes his flight to earth,
To view the region of his birth.
    O, grand is the hymn that peals through space,
As Earth proceeds on her endless race!   140
A hero-story that knows no end,
And aspirations that upward tend;
Yet, mixed with joyful and holy notes,
A wail of despair and sorrow floats;
For sorrow and sin on earth must dwell,
Though earth is falsely esteemed a hell,
For ever the joy outweighs the pain;
Thus Earth's is a mingled, moving strain.
    They saw the plain where in fight they died,
But over it now no armies ride: 150
They learn their country has gained the fight,
And put the legions of foes to flight.
    Then came the mundane Ruler near:
"My words of council, children, hear,
You cannot reach the Centre,
    And wherefore should you strive,
For duties still await you,
    As when on earth alive.

Return, my children, to the sun,
  And serve its Ruler well;   160
And should he so command you,
  Return with me to dwell:
For signs unnumbered now appear,
That speak a brighter Future here."
  "We will go to the sun as you bid us," replied
The meek-minded Arthur; but Michael then cried,
"I swear that none shall turn me back
Upon my great and holy track;
And save Alcyone's, no King,
Shall e'er forbid my wandering.   170
'Tis from the solar realms we come,
To seek in space a brighter home."
  "Beside you," Arthur said, "I fly
To any region of the sky."
  The angel blessed them ere they sped
Where Michael's inclination led;
And Michael exclaimed, "I will never stay more,
Until I arrive at that wonderful shore,
Where Alcyone only for ever shall sway
The Sceptre that governs the whole Milky Way!" 180

PART III. **ALCYONE.**

As Michael resolved, they trod no more,
How lovely soe'er, upon any shore:
The planets superior Michael passed by,
Unheeding, his thoughts in the fathomless sky;
But Arthur, who listened more closely, could hear
The exquisite music that rang from each sphere:
Increasing in grandeur away into space,
As each from the sun was removed in its place.
By millions of suns the adventurers passed,
Each system exceeding in glory the last,   10
Yet each in its place was as needful as all;
Nor any were useless, though pallid or small.
Then through the dark paths of their measureless track,
Went Michael unfearing, nor ever turned back,
Away through the ocean of ether that lies
Throughout the whole Kosmos, wherever he flies.
"Away to Alcyone's brightness!
    No distance my path shall oppose;
And lo, where its glory transcendant,
    Through regions all measureless flows!"   20
O'er all the light from every sun,
    Came now one dazzling ray
That cast all meaner worlds in shade,
    To guide them on their way.
And now before them full in sight,
Appears a world of liquid light.
Ten thousand suns of Sirius' size,
Would seem as darkness to the eyes,
That once had seen the glory thrown
Around it by that star alone!   30

No solid centre has that sun,
At which they stopped, their journey done;
But streams of dazzling vapours roll
In oceans huge, from pole to pole:
The fluid mortals Odyle call,
The least ethereal of them all!
  Ten thousand, thousand worlds of light,
Are whirled around their Centre bright; ·
And now can they perceive the reins
Of light that bind them in their chains;   40
And they can hear the glorious song,
That every world, (or faint or strong,)
Lends to the Music of the Spheres;
In harmony to heavenly ears,
Howe'er discordant it may sound
To those who tread terrestrial ground.
And see in all his glory here,
Alcyone's own King appear!
"O King o'er Alcyone ruling!
  Our journey of glory is done: 50
We have flown from the verge of Creation,
  To worship the Innermost Sun!"
"I am not the King of Creation,
  For numberless suns are more bright:
And sought you the Centre for aions,
  It never would dawn on your sight.
O Michael, your pride shall debar you
  For long from the Vision divine:
The sight of the King of Creation,
  Shall not, till you seek him, be thine!   60
'Tis not in these regions of splendour,
  You seek for the Universe Soul:

But seek him, O proud one, within you,
 And then mayst thou look for the goal!
And Arthur, so humble and trusting,
 Has worshipped more truly than thou;
And God can draw nearer to Arthur,
 For lo, he appears to him now!"
He looked at Arthur, and he saw
A sight that filled his soul with awe,
For Arthur's face became so bright
That Michael could not bear the sight:
And under that diviner ray,
The Central Sun's intensest day,
Grew pale and wan. Their journey done,
The twain that distant star had won;
And lo, when Michael raised his head,
The glory of the star had fled,
And in the sun again they stood,
Beside the flashing lightning flood.
 Then said the Ruler of the Sun,
"Your dream of Central Suns is done;
But o'er two meaner planets reign,
Nor seek for Central Suns again:
But in your hearts the King adore,
So vainly sought in space before,
Amid those realms of radiant light,
Where shines Alcyone, so bright
You thought it might that Monarch be,
Whom outer eyes may never see;
And learn to feel, throughout the Whole,
One Omnipresent, Primal Soul!"

BIRDS OF PARADISE.

When these birds were first brought to Europe, their history
was supposed to be as here narrated.

BENEATH the glowing Orient skies,
Where nutmeg, date, and palm-trees rise,
Amid those groves of varied green,
The Birds of Paradise are seen,

At times, when from their Eden bowers,
They come to taste the Eastern flowers,
Footless they soar aloft in air,
And hatch the eggs they upward bear.

But that bright clime is not their home,
Nor the blue air through which they roam,
For nowhere upon all earth's breast,
But Eden, do they deign to rest.

And never mortal captured one,
But happiness around him shone,
Reflected from those regions bright,
Where dwell they in eternal light.

For never quits the sun the skies,
And neither clouds nor storms arise,
In Eden, where those birds alight,
Returning from their earthly flight.

14

THE POET.

He sat in his lonely cottage,
  And though he was poor and old,
He knew that the words he uttered,
  Were brighter than gems or gold.
He stood on the topmost mountain,
  And looked o'er the glittering sea:
"Like ocean the thoughts that fill me
  Are boundless and pure and free.

"I've sung of the stars above me,
  Whose distance no tongue can tell,
And I, in the cause of virtue,
  Have sung of the fabulous Hell.
I trust in Eternal Goodness,
  That all who have ever been,
Shall meet in the worlds around me
  From evil for ever clean.

"What though I am poor and lonely?
  No bonds shall confine my soul!
Though earth should be torn asunder,
  While ages eternal roll,
My soul is not bound to ages!
  For ever when Space and Time
Have quitted their hold upon me,
  Shall mine be a holier clime!"

He stood on the topmost mountain,
  And looked o'er the verdant plain:
"This sight I have viewed so often,
  I shall not see here again.

My chains shall be snapped asunder:
 I have to myself been true,
And those who with truth can speak it,
 Scenes brighter than these shall view."

He stood on the topmost mountain,
 And turned to the city below:
"The wonders of human nature,
 No poet on earth shall know.
I've sung of all human passions;
 Of war, and of love, and of hate:
No evil shall last for ever,
 If man will endure and wait.

"The chains that have most oppressed me,
 Are Matter and Time and Space:
I speak, and I feel them loosened:
 Thank God I have run my race!"
He stood on the topmost mountain,
 Then sank on the frozen sod:
His duty on earth was over;
 His spirit returned to God!

THE NORNIR.

The three Fates of the Northern Mythology, Past, Present, and Future, sit by the Fountain of the Past, above the rainbow, weaving the fates of men.

THREE brothers have climbed the rainbow,
    And stand by the ruling Powers,
Whom Æsir and men must worship
    As Queens of the passing hours.

The first has exclaimed to Urthur,
    "O grant me the year that's gone,
And I will seize hold on Fortune!"
    The Norna spun sternly on.

"Unhappy is he, O mortal,
    Who makes a request of me!
The Queen of the vanished ages,
    Can never do aught for thee.

"Not even the mighty Othin
    Dare ask for a day that's flown:
The time that on earth we grant thee,
    Alone canst thou make thine own!"

The next has addressed Verthandi:
    "O Queen, at thy throne I bow:
I care not for aught save pleasure,
    And long let me live as now!"

"Unhappy is he, O mortal,
    Who makes a request of me!
The Queen of the passing ages,
    Can never do aught for thee.

"With Skulda abides the future:
  To men she decrees the right;
Then fear her, and ne'er offend her,
  For none may oppose her might.

"For Fenrir shall rend his fetters,
  And Othin himself must die ;
And none of the mighty Æsir,
  Can ever with Skulda vie!"

The third stands before veiled Skulda:
"Who like unto thee is Queen?
The face that thy veil yet hideth,
  Nor Asa nor man has seen!

"I've lived in thy sight from childhood,
  And this do I ask of thee,
That I, in the Hall of Gimli,
  The glory of Baldur see!"

"He only is wise, O mortal,
  Who places in me his trust;
The Queens of the Past and Present,
  Care nought for your race of dust.

"Nor Asa nor man is happy
  Who does not confide in me:
When Baldur returns from Helheim,
  His glory he shares with thee!"

THE FUTURE.

Written after reading Luke Burke's speculations in no. 3 of
the periodical of that name.

WHAT is this earth on which we tread,
  And what the radiant sun,
Round which the planets and the earth,
  In yearly courses run?

This earth it is a living thing,
  And slowly shall recede
For countless ages, from the sun,
  Which earth no more shall heed.

Yet think not that the earth shall freeze,
  When distant from the sun:
The glory that the sun displays,
  Shall earth itself put on!

Then shall the chain that binds the earth
  Be snapped for evermore:
And she shall rove in endless space,
  Through seas without a shore.

And round the new and brilliant star
  Shall planets swiftly run;
And every planet, in its turn,
  Grow up into a sun.

And 'mid the ever-burning lights
  Shall forms celestial move;
Whose eyes no tear shall ever dim, —
  Whose only thought is Love.

And be this true or be it false,
  Eternity shall show:
But all we learn assures us still
  How little man can know.

The truth, and truth alone shall stand:
  Whate'er is false must fall;
And whatsoe'er we think or speak,
  Affects not truth at all.

THALASSA.

The silent depths of the ocean sleep,
Unmoved by the storms that o'er them sweep:
The waves above may be white with foam,
And sea-birds dart o'er their restless home:
But crimson seaweeds in beauty wave
O'er rocks that the ocean currents lave,
Where never a sound of earth is heard;
No hum of insect or song of bird:
But worms of silver, and green, and gold,
And creatures whose forms no pen has told,
With rainbow gleams in their shining hair,
Are living by all unnoticed there.
The depths of the sea no man may tread,
And all is darkness and silence dread.
The sunlight becomes an ocean-green,
In regions no human eye has seen.
    A youth stands high on a rock, and looks
Down into the ocean's crystal nooks:
He sees the bright fishes that glide along,
He hears like a voice the murmuring song,
That cries, "The waters are cool and clear;
Descend amid them, and do not fear!"
    He loves the ocean by which he stands,
And fain would range through its deepest lands;
And once when a child he trod the shore,
He saw a face he forgot no more.
He's dived as deep as a man can dive,
And come from the ocean depths alive.
He's swum through the heaviest breaker's roar,
And swum till his strength availed no more;

But ever he turns to earth again,
To hope to dwell in the sea is vain;
Aud when he can swim no more, he takes
His stand on a rock where ocean breaks,
And looks on ocean till shore and sea
By evening blended, from vision flee:
Yet never he sees the sea-maid rise,
Whose form is ever before his eyes.

    He leaned from the rock whereon he stood,
And dipped his hands in the crystal flood;
He dipped his hands in the ocean brine, —
"O would that a mermaid's love were mine!
O would that the ancient tales were true;
And under the sunlit waters blue,
That I might wander, and never more
Return to the earth I trod before!"

    A murmur around him everywhere,
A music in earth and sea and air;
The waves below him are cleft in twain,
A path is carved in the trackless main;
And lo, in her peerless majesty,
Thalassa, Queen of the azure sea!
Before him the maid he loves appears,
Enraptured, her longed-for tones he hears:
"O child of man, I have heard thy prayer,
And worthy art thou my throne to share!
The waters shall hurt thee not. O come,
And make in the deep thy future home!"

    One look at the earth, one glance to heaven, —
His sole farewell in that look was given!
He sprang from the rock on which he stood,
And deeply sank in the azure flood.

The sunlit waters around him plashed,
And louder against the rocks they dashed,
But down in the waters sank the boy.
His heart possessed with a wondrous joy.
He stood in a matchless hall of red,
Where corals adorn the ocean bed,
And noiselessly gliding to and fro
Around him the loveliest fishes go.
His wish is gained, and the deepest sea
At length to a mortal's tread is free;
And while he gazes around, beside
Behold Thalassa, his future bride!
Her sea-green tresses are all unbound,
And sweeping loose till they touch the ground;
Her face is calm, but it seems to wear
A hopeless look of resigned despair.
But why should the Ocean Queen be sad
Beside the youth whom her love makes glad?
    "O youth," she cried, "I have called thee here,
To warn thee the ocean depths to fear.
We're soulless, and save by mortal's love
We never can rise to heaven above.
But even for immortality,
I ask not for such a gift from thee.
This wondrous blessing can ne'er be mine
Unless a man should his soul resign.
My race will entice a youth away,
And then for his soul with tears they pray;
And if he grant it, then woe indeed!
The mermaid from ocean's depths is freed,
But leaves the youth in the ocean deep,
Where body and soul for aye must sleep.
Three kisses confer this priceless boon,

An awful gift to bestow so soon!
Away from my halls, O mortal, fly
Or body and soul alike must die;
And never again permit my race
To lure thee into my dwelling-place.
I love thee, and therefore bid thee flee,
And warn thee not to remember me!"
   "Not so, Thalassa!" exclaimed the youth,
"If what you tell me indeed be truth
More wretched are you by far than I,
Away to the realms of glory fly, —
And wander amid eternal bliss,
My soul I give you,—receive my kiss!
I do not think that the God of heaven,
Permits a soul from its body riven,
To sleep in eternal gloom for ever:
We meet this instant on high, or never!
O Queen of the Sea, you refuse my love,
Although by its might you rise above.
I will not be so unworthy thee
As not to resolve to set thee free!"
   He clasped in his arms the weeping maid,
To die for her he was not afraid;
And solemnly gave each mystic kiss
That opened the gates of endless bliss.
O wonder! the coral hall is fled,
And neither the youth nor maid is dead.
The ocean waters are far away:
They stand in a world of endless day.
And now they wander through realms on high
Where none who enter shall ever die.
Their holy love could no magic sever,
And sundered they shall not be for ever!

QUEEN GUNHILDA.

Founded on a beautiful Norwegian tradition related by Grimm.
See Keightley's Fairy Mythology, p. 130.

PART I.

WHERE frowns a lonely island,
    A giant-king appears,
Whose magic trumpet's echoes,
    The boldest seaman fears.

Each morn he takes his trumpet,
    And sounds a fearful blast,
And every ship it reaches,
    Against the rocks is cast.

And when the ship is shattered,
    The sailors make for land,
But form the food of giants,
    If e'er they touch the strand.

The giant-queen, Gunhilda,
    In vain for men may plead,
For Andfind, ever ruthless,
    Condemns them all to bleed.

"All other boons, my fairest,
    I pray thee ask of me,
But cease thy prayer for mercy,
    For that can never be.

"For Olaf sails against us,
    Tremendous in his might;
Nor can we hope for safety,
    Unless 'tis sought in flight.

QUEEN GUNHILDA. **221**

"I will not flee before him,
 But drink of human gore,
And strengthened thus for combat,
 Will fight him on the shore."

Again he sounds his trumpet.
 A ship appears in sight,
Whose sails against the vapours
 Expand all snowy white.

And where the deck grows narrow,
 Behold St. Olaf stand:
His sailors ranged behind him,
 A cross in every hand!

The giants fled in terror,
 For him they dreaded more
Than e'en the crushing hammer,
 That Thor possessed of yore.

All, save the mighty Andfind,
 Who arms him for the strife:
"O, shun this dreadful Olaf!"
 Exclaims his weeping wife.

"Not so!" the giant answered:
 "For one I dare not name,
Has sent his servant hither
 To spread his holy fame.

"I do not fear St. Olaf:
 His life is in my hand;"
He looked, and saw the vessel
 Come sailing to the land.

Through land as if through water,
  The ship pursued its course;
It ground the rocks to powder,
  So wondrous was its force!

The giant rushed to meet it,
  And hurl it from the shore,
But soon his footsteps faltered,
  His strength availed no more:

For Olaf cried in anger,
  "Thou hast opposed to-day,
The holy might of Olaf:
  Become a stone for aye!"

As Olaf spoke, the giant
  Stood rooted to the ground;
And, when the curse was ended,
  A mighty rock was found.

Then rose Gunhilda weeping,
  And she to Olaf spoke;
"Have mercy on me, Olaf,
  And let the spell be broke!"

"Not thine thy husband's vices",
  The holy Olaf said:
"But list what hard conditions,
  Avail to wake the dead!

"Thy life may last for ages,
  But death must come at last;
And do not hope the future
  Will e'er revive the past.

"On Christmas Eves 'tis granted,
  Thou mayst thy lord recall;
But when the day is ended,
  His doom again shall fall.

"But every time he wakens,
  A hundred years I take,
And from the term assigned thee,
  The hundred years I break.

"But if when thus awakened,
  The name of Christ he hears,
No sacrifice shall wake him."
  Gunhilda dried her tears.

"O thanks, most noble Olaf!
  How gladly I for love
Will pay the price thou askest,
  And hope for nought above!"

Then once again St. Olaf
  Departed on his way,
While Queen Gunhilda murmured,
  "How light a price to pay!"

PART II.

To rocks and caverns fleeing,
  The dwarfs and giants hide;
For Christian ships are cleaving
  A path through every tide.

On Christmas Eves, Gunhilda
  Awakes the mighty dead:
And, since his transformation,
  Five hundred years have fled.

But never dares Gunhilda
  Permit a ship to land:
She stands upon the island,
  And warns them from the strand.

Two lovers in the night-time
  Have fled away from home,
And hoping scarce for safety,
  They tempt the ocean's foam,

And Orm and Aslog, flying
  From Aslog's father's hate,
Direct their fragile vessel
  Towards the island straight.

But evermore a whirlpool
  Diverts them from the track,
And when they near the island,
  It drives them headlong back.

"God aid us!" Orm in terror
  Exclaimed, "we ne'er can gain
The desert isle before us,
  But perish in the main!"

No more Gunhilda's magic
  Avails to stay the skiff:
It rushes through the water,
  Where lowest stoops the cliff.

Now Orm and Aslog, climbing
  The higher cliffs, behold
A stately palace standing,
  That shines with ruddy gold:

And by the door, Gunhilda,
  In human form appears,
"And now, ye weary strangers,
  Abandon all your fears.

"Secure from every danger,
  My house shall be your own,
But 'tis on these conditions
  I shelter you, alone:

"No holy word must ever
  Within these walls resound,
Nor may you mark with crosses,
  The ceilings, walls, or ground.

"On Christmas Eves I ask you,
  Resign the house to me;
And, if your lives you value,
  The palace then you'll flee.

"But if you will not leave it,
  Here, in this upper room,
Remain, nor watch my movements,
  For fear of dreadful doom!"

PART III.

On Christmas Eve Gunhilda
  Has hid her guests away,
For now the giant Andfind
  Again beholds the day.
And Orm and Aslog listen,
  And view the feast below,
Where Andfind and Gunhilda
  Their ancient glory show.

By countless dwarfs surrounded
  Behold the royal pair,
Amid their faithful subjects
  Awhile dispel their care.

But with the noise awakened,
  Doth Aslog's infant cry:
"O cheer thee up, my baby,
  For Christ is ever nigh!"

Then from the guests assembled,
  A cry of terror broke,
And all the lights they vanished
  In clouds of sulphur smoke.

Next morning Queen Gunhilda
  To Orm and Aslog came:
Clad all in deepest mourning
  Appeared that noble dame.

"No more can I for ever
  Awake my husband dead;
And by your interference,
  My happiness has fled.

"As though I crushed an egg-shell,
  Could I destroy your lives:
And I, before unhappy,
  Most wretched am of wives.

"But since by heedless speaking,
  You caused this woe to me,
Aslog, the worst offender,
  I will not punish thee.

"I give ye all my treasures,
  And on some desert shore,
Will wait the destined moment,
  To meet my lord once more.

"And if like other giants,
  We both are doomed to Hell,
'Twere happier than for either
  In Heaven alone to dwell!"

Thus spoke the Queen Gunhilda,
  And raised her tearful eyes;
But now a heavenly vision,
  Fills all with strange surprise.

A strain of holy music
  Assails the listening ear;
And yet the Queen Gunhilda
  Betrays no signs of fear.

And hark how angel voices
  Repeat one holy strain:
"Bow down, O earthly princes,
  For Christ descends to reign!"

"Well done, O Queen Gunhilda!"
   A herald angel cries:
"Well hast thou borne thy trial,
   And won a heavenly prize!

"God grants thee Heaven for ever,
   Nor grants it but to thee;
For, succoured by thy virtues,
   Shall Andfind with thee be!"

Thereat the angels vanished,
   And as the vision fled,
Gunhilda clasped the statue,
   And sank upon it dead!

HERACLES AND IPHICLES.

HERACLES.

I come from the chase with my spear all red:
The lion lies in the forest dead.
He sprang from his lair to seize the man
Who dared to roam in the haunts of Pan:
Unmoved I waited the mighty foe:
I raised my spear, and I laid him low.

IPHICLES.

The joys of the chase delight not me;
The face of danger I will not see;
And why should we tempt the wrath of Zeus,
By fighting a scourge his will lets loose?
So long as he grants me clothes and food,
I look on fame as an idle good.

HERACLES.

I sought to climb the Olympian hill;
Through clouds and thunder I struggled still,
And over a torrent wild I stood,
A hundred fathoms above the flood:
Unmoved, though scarcely my foot could bide,
So narrow its rest on the mountain's side!

IPHICLES.

O brother, my heart is faint and weak,
To hear the perils of which you speak.
O wherefore wilt thou attempt a strife
That none can hope to succeed with life?
Olympus is crowned with endless snow,
And perils guard it that none can know.

HERACLES.

I climbed the mount 'mid the thunder's roar,
The storm around me increasing more,
And utter darkness around me fell,
A darkness intense as that of Hell;
And still 'mid the awful gloom I strove
To climb to the blissful seats above.

IPHICLES.

O brother beware, and let the hill
Arise in its virgin glory still!
The home of the Gods be sure is vain
For e'en thy valour to hope to gain.
Lay by the unrest and discontent,
That must such desperate schemes invent!

HERACLES.

I came at length to a lower peak,
But not the palace I went to seek.
Above me, Olympus reared its head:
Below, the tempest was raging dread;
And 'mid the tumult I stood and smiled,
And wondered if Zeus beheld his child?

IPHICLES.

The father of all is Zeus indeed;
Yet grants he to none their danger's meed,
And better to wait till Zeus shall send
The night that never shall know an end,
Than venture by dangers dread to call
From Heaven the death foredoomed to all.

HERACLES.

Amid the thunder I heard a voice:
"Descend, O hero, rejoice, rejoice!

Olympus thou mayst in time attain,
But only by years of toil and pain.
O never falter or turn or flee,
And Zeus shall bestow his strength on thee,
And grant thee courage and skill to fight
The foes that assail thy charmèd might!"

IPHICLES.

Beware the deceit! Are we not told,
That fled for aye is the Age of Gold?
And well may it be that Zeus would lead
Thy dread presumption to woe indeed.

HERACLES.

Sayst thou the Gods would attempt to kill
A man who ascends their holy hill?
Had fear assailed me indeed I know,
The lightnings round me had laid me low.
I do not distrust the Gods above:
A dauntless hero they guard and love.

IPHICLES.

I go my way, and do thou go thine,
For mad thou art, or distraught with wine!

CHEIRON.

Lo, now we know by the paths ye choose,
The son of man, and the son of Zeus!

SIR BEDIVERE.

KING Arthur has passed from human sight:
The Dragon Standard no more in fight,
Shall lead his knights to again oppose
The armies of heathen Saxon foes;
And none of his noble knights again
Shall ever enter the battle-plain,
For well they stood by their master's side,
And fought till they all like heroes died.
Sir Bedivere was the only one,
That lived to behold the morrow's sun!
The hero returned to Carduel,
The town that King Arthur loved so well.
He met a horseman who rode with speed
To warn the knights of the city's need.
"Woe to thee, Sir Bedivere,
For an army's marching here!
Soon the town shall glow with flame:
Who the Saxon's wrath can tame?
And though Modred be o'erthrown,
Arthur must defend his own.
Legions more of Arthur's foes,
Round the walls of Carduel close.
God send Arthur and his host,
To defend our town and coast!"
"Arthur thou shall see no more:
In a ship he left the shore."
"Where are thy companions gone?"
"They have perished every one!"
"Hasten thou, and let us lead
Forth, in our extremest need,

All who warlike arms can wield;
Wilt thou head them in the field?"
"All are gone save I alone,
Of the knights round Arthur's throne:
Future histories shall tell,
Bedivere a hero fell!"
    Then rode they to the city-gate,
And all the Britons armed them straight;
And eager cries from the troops arose,
That Bedivere should attack their foes.
    Sir Bedivere still for a moment stood,
Then raised his sword that was red with blood,
And swore an oath that the Saxon foe,
The edge of a British sword should know:
Nor ever his hand his sword should leave,
Nor cease the heads of his foes to cleave;
Nor e'er should that sword be sheathed again,
But deeper and deeper should rust its stain,
So long as a Saxon foe could say,
"The land I stand on is mine to-day!"
    With that he assailed the heathen band,
(His sword of vengeance was in his hand:)
A Knight of the Table Round they knew,
And all assemble to meet the foe,
And rush like a whirlwind round the knight:
O well and bravely he bore the fight!
Fiercer press the countless foes,
But the knight strikes harder blows,
And whene'er the ranks divide,
Turns Sir Bedivere aside,
Ever seeks the thickest fray,
Searching but for foes to slay.

He raised a rampart of heathen dead,
Before the town, and the Saxons fled.
　Then sank the knight among his foes:
From three deep wounds his life-blood flows;
When parts the ground 'mid an earthquake's roar,
And Morgan's boat appears once more:
But empty now of human form,
It sails amid the battle's storm,
Along a stream which parts the knight
From those who beat him down in fight,
And where no river flowed before,
In Arthur's days, or days of yore.
He dragged himself on board with pain,
And lo, his wounds are healed again!
Across the Saxon country,
　The wondering traveller speeds,
And through the gloomy forests,
　Marshes, and flowery meads.
The ocean soon he reaches,
　And Bedivere looks round;
Behind him in the distance
　Afar is British ground;
When lo, the shores of Brittany,
　Does Bedivere behold;
He passes through the forests,
　The scenes of legends old:
And now in utter darkness
　The waters drive the boat,
And far below the forests,
　Does Bedivere now float.
Deep down beneath a mountain,
　Behold the light appear;

And Bedivere looks onward
  In wonder free from fear.
A lamp that burns for ever
  Sheds light amid the gloom;
He sees a rock of marble,
  And reads, 'tis Merlin's tomb!
Stand up, O Bedivere, and take
  The magic horn that lies
Beside the tomb where Merlin sleeps,
  And bid the dead arise!
He sounded loud the magic horn,
  And hears the Prophet's voice:
"The promised hero sounds the horn,
  And Merlin must rejoice.
Thirty years of deadly gloom,
Dwelt I in my living tomb,
Till the knight of prophecy,
Comes to bid my fetters fly.
Fetters Vivien's hand hath spun,
Are not easily undone!
Now my longed-for bliss I see;
Avalon awaiteth me!
Arthur shall not tread again
Earthly ground in joy or pain,
Till his war-tormented land,
Foremost in the world shall stand;
Till the steam shall drive the car
Over regions near and far;
And across the stormy main,
Where the winds and tides are vain,
Even to impede the boat
Steam and iron force to float:

Till the lightning's flash shall bear
Spoken converse everywhere;
And in war the missiles cast
Are not those of ages past,
But for arrows' piercing pain,
Falls a deadly iron rain,
Crushing armour, crushing bone;
Ships of iron, walls of stone.
When King Arthur's latest knight
Wounded falls in fiercest fight,
He shall be conveyed to me,
And at length shall set me free.
When the thirty years are flown,
Then the third and loudest tone
Of the magic horn shall rend
Marble tomb from end to end!"

Thrice he sounds that horn of doom:
Can its echoes pierce a tomb?
Loud and long the hero blew,
And the horn in pieces flew,
And the marble burst in twain:
Rises Merlin once again.

"Now I fly to Avalon,
For my night of woe is done:
Seek it with me, Bedivere,
Else thou canst not enter there!
Walls of flame and walls of ice,
Guard that earthly Paradise;
Walls of water, rock, and sand,
Compass it on every hand:
Yet in this boat can we enter
    Eden, whence Adam once fell:

Arthur abides at its portals,
  Waiting the call of a spell.
Avalon's part of that Eden:
  Thence in his pride shall he ride,
(Not till his country most needs him)
  Hundreds of knights at his side!"
They climbed the boat, and swift it flew
  Through seas and deserts, rocks and ice,
Volcanoes, whirlpools, till at length
  They neared the bounds of Paradise.
They left the boat, and Merlin led
  Sir Bedivere ashore,
And to the castle they advanced,
  And passed the open door:
And in the castle hall, behold
Arrayed in purple, silver, gold,
King Arthur, with the noble knights,
Who fought with him so many fights.
  Then Morgan spoke to Merlin:
"Be Vivien now forgot;
For thou hast come, O Prophet,
Where treachery is not.
Welcome to thee, Bedivere:
Avalon no foes come near.
Last of Carduel's hero-band,
By King Arthur take thy stand,
Till some hero grasp the blade,
Owned by Arthur, undismayed;
Sound a magic horn, and call
Hence King Arthur's heroes all!"

238

ERRATA.

P. 11, l. 288, for "an" read "on."

P. 14, l. 384, for "disoheyd" read "disobeyed."

P. 31, l. 902 for "inneestahn" read „Jinneestahn."

P. 92, l. 841, for "haud" read "hand."

P. 93, l. 868, for "tumed" read "turned."

P. 99, l. 1059, for "than" read "that."

P. 116, l. 1561, for "thou will" read "thou wilt."

P. 125, l. 1842, for "Front" read "From."

P. 138, l. 69, for "tought" read "taught."

P. 158, l. 38, for "witheld" read "withheld."

P. 166, l. 275, for "Voiee" read "Voice."

P. 181, n. 7, last line, for "ore" read "are."

P. 182, bottom line, for "o" read "to."

P. 184, n. 33, l. 2, for "in placed" read "is placed."

P. 187, n. 72, l. 7, for "consistant" read "consistent."

P. 195, l. 7, for "froms" read "forms."

P. 203, l. 117, for "For" read "Far."

P. 204, l. 154, for "council" read "counsel."

P. 220, l. 3, from top, for "Fuiry" read "Fairy."

THE END.

+